No horsing

"Jordan and I want to [...] on horseback!" Molly blur[...]

"Hmm, I'm not sure Jordan is ready for that." Mama frowned a little.

"No, really, it was Jordan's idea. She wants to try it," Molly insisted. Was this a conspiracy? Had she and Madison planned to totally put me on the spot like this?

Then I saw Mama's face. It was lit up like a sunrise. She was *glowing*. There was really no other word for it. Instead of giving me the *Jordan, I'm so worried about you* look, she gave me something else I've hardly ever seen. The *Madison, I'm so proud of you* look.

If I had just announced that I'd discovered a cure for cancer and that I was marrying Prince William, she couldn't have been happier.

"Honey, really? You want to try jumping a horse?" Mama asked.

Now Mama, Eric, Eda, Molly, and Madison all stood around me in a semicircle. All eyes were on me. Staring. Waiting.

What else could I do?

"Yeah, I guess so," I heard myself say. "I mean, I actually want to try it. I'm going to jump a horse this summer."

One Summer. One Sleepaway Camp.
Three Thrilling Stories!

Summer Camp Secrets

How far will Kelly
go to hold on to
her new friends?

What happens when Judith
Ducksworth decides to
become JD at camp?

Can Darcy and
Nicole's friendship
survive the summer?

Summer Camp Secrets

FEARLESS

by
Katy Grant

ALADDIN
New York   London   Toronto   Sydney

In memory of my sister Nan.

You often tried to tell me what to do,
but you were also my biggest fan.

ALADDIN
An imprint of Simon & Schuster Children's Publishing Division
1230 Avenue of the Americas, New York, NY 10020
First Aladdin paperback May 2010
Text copyright © 2010 by Katy Grant
All rights reserved, including the right of reproduction
in whole or in part in any form.
ALADDIN is a trademark of Simon & Schuster, Inc., and related logo is a registered trademark of Simon & Schuster, Inc.
For information about special discounts for bulk purchases, please contact Simon & Schuster Special Sales at 1-866-506-1949 or business@simonandschuster.com.
The Simon & Schuster Speakers Bureau can bring authors to your live event. For more information or to book an event contact the Simon & Schuster Speakers Bureau at 1-866-248-3049 or visit our website at www.simonspeakers.com.
The text of this book was set in Perpetua.
Manufactured in the United States of America 0612 OFF
10 9 8 7 6 5 4
Library of Congress Control Number 2009937539
ISBN 978-1-4169-9162-5
ISBN 978-1-4424-0606-3 (eBook)

Acknowledgments

For this book, more than any of the others so far, I was in dire need of assistance. It has been years since I have ridden a horse, and what little I do remember about my formal riding instruction is fuzzy around the edges. So I had to call on a number of experts to guide me. These are the wonderful people who heeded my call and gave their time so generously.

I want to thank Cara Thompson, the head of the riding program at my former summer camp, who has guided me from start to finish on this book. Cara has a BA in Equine Business Management and has served as both a barn manager and instructor at St. Andrews Presbyterian College. Cara read sample chapters in the middle of her busy summer of teaching campers, responded to countless e-mails, and provided me with the feedback I so desperately needed. Her great sense of humor and her expertise in riding instruction were absolutely invaluable to me as I wrote this book.

Many thanks also to Amanda Weaver, who had just returned from a summer abroad in Russia and was about to start her senior year at Arizona State University when I asked her to read the complete manuscript. Amanda proved to be an excellent editor who answered all of my many questions. Amanda first began riding lessons at age six, and she has competed on the ASU Equestrian Team. Recently she was certified as a Therapeutic Riding Instructor for riders with mental and physical disabilities. Without the help of these two amazing young women, I never would have been able to write about the technical aspects of riding and jumping.

I also want to thank Eric Loring for meeting me for lunch and telling me about his many experiences with riding, jumping, and owning horses. Eric and I met when I was still in the earliest stages of trying to discover Jordan's story, and he was candid in his discussion of his own fears about riding.

I am so grateful to all of you for being with me on this journey. Truly, I couldn't have done it without you!

CHAPTER 1

Sunday, June 15

There was really no reason why I should be nervous, but I was. And whenever I got nervous, I always felt it in my stomach. I kept reminding myself that today should be no big deal.

Mama, Eric, Madison, and I were outside in the driveway, packing the car with all our camp stuff at the ridiculously early hour of six thirty a.m. Who knew that the sun would even be up this early? It was—barely. But the whole world was draped in a soft half-light that made everything seem slightly unreal.

All of a sudden, I felt that cold sweat I'd felt so many times before.

"I'll be back in a sec," I told them. Luckily, the garage door was open. I raced inside to the bathroom and stood there panting for a few seconds. My upper lip was all broken out in beads of sweat. I had to concentrate really hard to keep my breakfast inside my stomach where it belonged, but at the moment, my Cheerios and apple juice were trying to rebel against me.

I grabbed a washcloth off the rack and ran it under the cold water. While I was wiping my face with it, Mama called to me through the closed door. "Jordan, honey? Are you throwing up?"

Did she always have to know every single disgusting detail of my life? "No! I'm washing my face!"

After a couple of seconds, I actually felt better, and the sick feeling passed. But when I opened the door, Mama was standing there, holding up the little bottle of Dramamine. "Do you need to take one of these?"

I frowned at her. "I don't know. Do you think I should?"

"Well, you know how windy those roads get really close to camp."

I sighed. "Okay. Don't tell Madison I almost threw up, all right? Tell her I was washing my face." I had a dream. A simple dream. I wanted to keep my stomach issues from becoming the viral video of the week. Was that asking too much?

"Ah, honey!" Mama rubbed my back. "Don't get so

nervous! You're an old pro this year! It's not like last year. You've got a lot of friends at camp now. And Molly will be with you, and Madison. And of course Eda, but try not to bother her today, because you know how busy Opening Day is for her."

I took the pill Mama held out for me and swallowed it with a gulp of water. Having her tell me I shouldn't get nervous made me feel even worse.

She was right. This was going to be my *second* summer at Camp Pine Haven, so why was I on the verge of regurgitating?

Mama has always said I have a "nervous stomach" because it doesn't take much to make me regurgitate. Of all the words for throwing up—vomit, puke, barf, hurl—I liked *regurgitate* the best. It sounded more . . . medical.

"I'm not nervous. I'm just . . . stressed," I told Mama, looking at my fingernails so I wouldn't have to see her concerned look. "You know—making sure I packed everything, all this rushing around . . ."

Madison and I were going to camp for a whole month, so there were five thousand details I had to worry about. Anytime some major event was going on—when we were leaving for a trip, or if it was the first day of school—it was like you could *feel* the stress in the air, crackling like electricity. At least I could.

"Well, if you're feeling okay now, Eric and Madison are waiting for us."

When we went outside, Maddy was leaning against the car with this know-it-all look on her face. Not quite a smile, but almost.

The first thing she said was, "Did you throw up?"

"No." I brushed past her and climbed into the backseat.

"I swear, Jordan, you're the only one I know who gets carsick before you even leave the driveway." She scooted in next to me.

"I did not throw up! And excuse me for not being born perfect like *some* people." I stared out my window at the snowball bush by the driveway so I could avoid looking at her.

"You're excused!" She said it all perky. She was always in a good mood. I slightly hated her for that personality flaw.

Being too perky and perfect were just about the only personality flaws my sister had. She was sixteen, she made straight As, she was the star of her field hockey team, and about thirty-seven different boys were in love with her. And *nothing* made her nervous.

Perfection in older sisters has been known to cause

regurgitation issues in younger sisters. I was fairly sure that medical studies had proven that.

Maddy fished through her purse, pulled out a stick of gum, and offered it to me. I shook my head. She unwrapped it and shoved it under my nose, but I ignored her. The snowball bush had my undivided attention.

Eric and Mama were climbing into the front seat.

Eric turned the engine on and peeked at us in the rearview mirror. "Ready, ladies?" My stepfather was the sweetest guy in the world. It drove him slightly crazy living in a houseful of females, but he always put up with it.

"Ready!" yelled perky, perfect Madison. She'd given up trying to get me to take the gum and was chewing it herself. We started backing out of the driveway.

We didn't have far to go, just down the street to my best friend Molly's house. Molly threw open the front door and raced down her steps the second we pulled in the driveway.

"Finally! I didn't think you'd ever get here!" She had her sleeping bag under one arm and her pillow under the other. Her parents came out, carrying Molly's trunk by the handles.

"Think we'll get all this gear in?" asked Molly's father when Eric opened our already full trunk. The two of them shifted the duffels, trunks, and bags around while Molly gave her mother one last hug.

Molly squeezed in between me and Madison. Good. We needed a barrier between us. Too bad the Great Wall of China wouldn't fit in the backseat.

"How many times did you throw up this morning?" she whispered.

"Zero! And I slightly hate you for even bringing it up," I whispered back.

Molly laughed. "See, you're getting better. I'm glad you didn't get sick. I almost called you to ask."

In lots of ways, Molly and I are complete opposites. She has brown eyes and super-straight brown hair cut really short and parted in the middle. I have blue eyes, and my blond hair is past my shoulders, with a little bit of curl to it. She's short and stocky; I'm taller and slimmer.

The fathers were finished packing the trunk, so they slammed it closed, and Molly's parents leaned into the open car door and took another ten minutes saying good-bye. Finally we were ready to leave.

After he got in, Eric turned around in the front seat and smiled at all of us. "Next stop, Camp Pine Haven for Girls!" He was the only one in the car who hadn't made a comment about my regurgitation issue. I loved him for that.

We backed out of Molly's driveway and headed down the street. My stomach felt completely normal now. Hopefully, it wouldn't turn on me later. It's truly sad when you can't even trust your own organs, but my stomach has betrayed me many times. I've learned the hard way to be suspicious of it.

Mama glanced over her shoulder at me. "Feeling okay, honey?" she asked with her forehead crinkled up in worry lines. "We'll turn the air conditioner on and get some cool air blowing on you, all right?"

I leaned my head back against the seat and closed my eyes. "I'm *fine*."

I hated the way everyone had to pay so much attention to me. But that was partly my fault for being so abnormal. I have never been good at dealing with new experiences, and it had been a really big deal for me to go away to summer camp in the first place.

At least no one had said anything about the "major meltdown" summer. That was one of the worst experiences of my life.

Two years ago when I was ten, I was all set to go to camp for the first time. Eda Thompson, one of Mama's best friends, is the director of Pine Haven, so how could my mother have two daughters and not send them to her best friend's summer camp?

Madison had started going to camp when she was eight, and she loved everything about Pine Haven. So of course, everyone expected me to be just like Madison, but I didn't want to go when I was eight. Or nine.

Finally when I was ten, I felt this huge amount of pressure to go. I didn't want to, but I knew Mama, Madison, and Eda were all expecting me to go, and they all kept saying, "Just wait till you get there. You'll love it!"

But about fifty different things worried me. It was for a whole month, so I knew I'd be homesick, even with Maddy there and with Eda looking out for me. I'd be sleeping in a strange bed, away from home. I'd have to swim in a lake that was really deep with water that was dark green and you couldn't see the bottom of it. There would be all these strange girls I wouldn't know. Maybe my counselor would be really mean.

So about a week before camp started, I had a slight meltdown.

Actually, it was more like a major meltdown.

I started crying and I didn't stop. I cried for about two whole days. Major, major waterworks.

Everyone tried to comfort me in various ways that did absolutely no good at all. And yes, there were some regurgitation episodes. Eventually Mama said, "Fine, you don't have to go. You can stay home and miss out on all the fun."

So I stopped crying and immediately felt better, but I could tell she was majorly disappointed in me. Half of me felt so incredibly relieved that I didn't have to go to camp, but the other half felt like the biggest failure in the world.

So last summer when I was eleven, I knew I couldn't back out of it again. Luckily, Molly had moved to our neighborhood at the beginning of fifth grade and we got to be best, best friends. She wanted to go with me last year, and she was so excited that she made me feel a lot better about camp, but I was still nervous in the beginning.

Molly elbowed me and grinned. "Just think, tomorrow we'll actually be riding horses again! I can't wait to see Merlin. I wonder if he'll remember me."

Molly and I loved horseback riding more than any other activity at Pine Haven. Listening to her talk about horses made me excited. Camp really was fun, even if I did get nervous about the first day.

"I wonder if Amber will be in our cabin," said Molly.

"I don't know, but Eda promised she'd put you and me together."

I felt a sinking feeling inside me when I said that.

Eda probably thought I would have another meltdown if Molly wasn't right by my side. Once you've had one meltdown, people keep expecting you to have additional ones.

Mama was always telling people, "Jordan is a little more cautious than Madison. Jordan needs a little more encouragement than Madison does. Jordan is more sensitive than Madison."

Translation: Madison is perfectly normal. Then there's my abnormal daughter.

Last summer I had managed to get through the whole month of camp without having a meltdown. But like that was a big deal.

This summer I had to do more than just survive camp. Last year, the day we got home, I heard Mama on the phone to Daddy, giving him a report of how things went. They've been divorced since I was five, but they still get along really well.

"Jordan survived!" I heard her telling him. Her voice sounded so relieved. "Yes, she made it through the whole session. I honestly thought Eda was going to call me and say we'd have to come get her, but she made it! She survived! Maddy? Oh, well, you know how Madison loves camp. She thrived, just like she always does."

After I'd overheard that conversation, I went to my

room and locked the door. I cried for an hour. *Jordan survived; Madison thrived.* It was a horrible rhyme stuck in my head that kept repeating itself over and over and over.

This summer, I couldn't just survive.

This summer, I wanted it to be my turn to thrive.

CHAPTER 2

Actually, last year when I heard that, I wasn't exactly sure what *thrive* meant. I knew it was something good, better than just surviving, so I looked it up. It means "to prosper or flourish; to grow vigorously." It also means "to progress toward a goal despite circumstances."

I stared out the window at the scenery blurring past us. I had to think of some kind of goal for this summer. Something that would show everyone that there wasn't anything wrong with me. Something that they would never expect from the queen of major meltdowns.

Molly and I were both sitting scrunched down with our heads leaning back on the seat. Madison was hypnotized by the music playing through her earbuds. In the front seat, Mama had laid her head on the seat rest, and I could tell she was asleep from the way her head rolled around.

Molly and I planned to sign up for riding lessons just like we did last summer, and that way we'd get to ride three times a week. We would definitely be spending more time at the stables than anywhere else. So . . . what kind of riding goal could I have?

"I bet we'll really become expert riders this year," I said to Molly suddenly.

She narrowed her eyes at me a little suspiciously. "You think so?"

"Sure, I mean, why not? We're not beginners anymore. We took lessons all last summer."

I had an idea about something I could do that would show everyone. But even thinking about it made my heart beat faster. It was scary and dangerous. But if I did it, everyone would be so surprised. And impressed.

"We might even work up to jumping," I said. Now my heart was hammering so fast it felt like I'd just run a hundred-meter dash.

Jumping? Was I really ready for something as advanced as jumping?

Molly stared at me with her mouth open for what seemed like one whole minute. "Who are you? And what have you done with my best friend who won't even jump off the high dive?"

I sighed with frustration. "A lot of people don't like to jump off the high dive," I insisted. One thing I really liked about Pine Haven was that the lake had only one diving board, a low dive—unlike the neighborhood pool we swam in. "Anyway, jumping a horse over a wall wouldn't be as scary as jumping off the high dive."

She looked directly at me like she was seeing me for the first time. "Seriously? You would really be willing to jump a wall on a horse?"

I wondered if she could hear my heart thumping, because it sure felt like the telltale heart that everyone in the whole car must be able to hear. *Boom, boom, boom, boom.*

First my stomach was completely unreliable. Now my heart was out of control. What next? My liver? Who knew what kinds of trouble a liver could get into?

I swallowed and took a deep breath. "I'll do it if you will," I told her.

"That's amazing! That's awesome! I would love to start jumping this summer!" Molly was practically screaming. She was so loud that Madison pulled her earbuds out.

"What are y'all talking about?" she asked.

Molly clutched Madison's arm excitedly. "Jordan says she wants to try jumping a horse this summer! She said she'd do it if I do it!"

Madison glanced at me with her eyebrows raised. "Jordan? Jordan who?"

I sat up straight in the seat. "What? You don't think I could do it?" I snapped at Maddy. "You don't think I'm good enough? Maybe I haven't been riding since I was a *two-year-old*, but I have been on a horse before."

Molly giggled in total disbelief. "Two? You've been riding horses since you were two?"

Madison smiled innocently at me. "Of course not. I was . . . three! Actually, I didn't start riding seriously at Pine Haven until I was eleven or twelve."

"How old were you when you jumped for the first time?" asked Molly. I was glad she'd asked, because I'd been wondering that myself.

Madison pressed her lips together. "Twelve. I think. Maybe." She shrugged. "I honestly can't remember."

Oh, really? She couldn't remember? Or did she just not want to say because she didn't want me to do something at a younger age than she'd done it?

Madison had learned to ride a two-wheeler when she was five. I'd learned when I was six. And a half. Madison started swimming lessons at four and was on a swim team by the time she was seven. I started swimming lessons when I was six, and finally, by the time I was ten, I was an okay swimmer.

I glanced at the back of Mama's head, propped on the headrest. She'd remember how old Madison was when she jumped a horse for the first time. She wrote down everything. There was even this chart in our baby books where she marked down the order we lost all our baby teeth in.

That was one thing I'd beaten Madison in. She'd lost her first tooth at five years and four months, and I'd lost my first one at five years and two months.

Whoop-de-do! I was almost positive that there wasn't a competitive tooth-losing event in the Olympics.

"You never answered my question," I said accusingly. "Do you think I could learn to jump or not?"

Madison leaned forward a little and looked past Molly at me. "Yeah, I think you *could* do it. But I don't know, Jordan. You know how you get about stuff like that."

Translation: I think you're too much of a wimp to actually go through with it.

"Well, maybe I'll surprise you. I'm going to learn how to jump this summer. It's something I really want to do."

My heart was racing again. What was I getting myself into? But there was something about the way that Madison looked at me. An *I'll believe it when I see it* look.

"Okay, whatever. Good luck with that," Madison said. She made a little snorting sound that wasn't quite a laugh before putting her earbuds back in.

At that moment, I wished more than anything I could be on the back of a horse, racing up to a five-foot-tall fence. My horse and I would go sailing over the top, and everything would be in slow motion, so I'd have a chance to turn and look at Madison standing there in the ring, watching me, her eyes the size of two dinner plates. I'd smile briefly at her and then turn forward, just before my horse and I made a graceful landing.

If only I could make my real life as perfect as my fantasies.

"This is great! I am *so* excited," Molly said, not even noticing how Madison had snubbed me and my whole plan.

"Yeah, I can't wait," I said, sliding down low in the seat again.

Maybe jumping was easier than I thought. Maybe it only looked scary and dangerous.

I squinted from the sunlight shining in through my window and gazed at the cars speeding past us on the interstate. It would've been a long, boring drive without Molly. She'd brought along some Mad Libs in her backpack, so those kept us entertained for more than an hour.

After a while, Eric cleared his throat and announced, "We're just about to enter North Carolina."

That made us all excited, because it meant we were that much closer to camp. But soon the steep mountain roads got very twisty and curvy. The Dramamine I'd taken earlier did the trick, though, and I didn't have to ask Eric to pull the car over, luckily. I patted my stomach gratefully. You're supposed to reward bad dogs for good behavior, so maybe all it needed was a stomach whisperer to make it behave.

"There's the sign! I see it!" Molly shouted. Madison pulled out her earbuds, and a big smile spread across her face. I sat forward in my seat. After a long three-hour car ride, we were all happy to finally be here.

Mama woke up right on cue and looked at the three of us in the backseat. "Everyone excited?"

The wooden sign by the road said CAMP PINE HAVEN FOR GIRLS, EST. 1921. It was hard to believe that Pine Haven was that old, but it was. And driving into camp sort of felt like we were going back in time, because everything had a rustic, woodsy feel.

We turned onto the road that led into camp. Overhead, the tree branches arched across the road and met in the middle, so it was like driving through a tunnel lined with green leaves. There was the dirt path that led through the woods to the riflery range, and then we rounded a corner and came out into wide-open space.

We passed the archery range on the left—basically an open field with colorful straw targets at the far end—and to the right of us was the lake. I smiled when I saw it. Sunlight danced on the water, and even though it was completely empty of people right now, I knew that in a few hours girls would be lined up, waiting to take swim tests.

"I can already feel how cold that water is!" I whispered to Molly.

"Just think of all the baby tadpoles swimming around in there now!" she added.

Last summer, I'd been ultra nervous about swimming in a lake. At first the cold, cold water was majorly shocking, but once you got used to it, you realized just how refreshing it actually felt. And the tadpoles didn't bother us if we didn't bother them. It was fun to watch them grow tiny arms and legs and change into little frogs as the days went by.

Overlooking the lake was Senior Lodge, a big stone

building with a wooden porch across the front of it. Eda had told us that except for a few repairs over the years, most of the lodges, cabins, and buildings looked the same as when they had first been built years and years ago.

Behind the lodge, hidden among the trees, were the Senior cabins for the oldest girls, thirteen and up. Molly and I were Middlers, the ten- to twelve-year-old age group. The youngest group was the Juniors, nine and under.

As we got to the center of camp, we could see people walking around, but we were definitely ahead of the huge crowds of Opening Day.

"It's so awesome that we got here early. I hope I'm the first CAT here. I'll get the best bed in the Perch," Madison announced.

"The CATs are so cool! I can't even believe I know one of them personally." Molly flashed a big grin at Madison, who was doing her best not to gloat over the fact that she was one of the elite this year—a Counselor Assistant in Training. The CATs practically ran Pine Haven in some ways, because they got to plan lots of evening programs and assemblies. Since they were sixteen, they weren't old enough to be counselors yet, but they weren't considered campers anymore.

"I guess we'll have to help you move into the Perch,

won't we?" I said casually. "You've got lots of stuff to carry, so just leave it to Molly and me."

"Ha ha, nice try. Stay away or you'll set off the alarm system," she warned us.

"There's no alarm system!" Molly yelled.

"How would you know? You've never seen the inside of it. And you won't for another four years."

The CATs were so privileged they had their own cabin, deep in the woods behind the dining hall. A lot of newbies didn't even know where it was. None of the campers were allowed to go inside it or even go near there. It was called the Perch because it was high up on a hill, and cats like to sleep on high perches.

Eric pulled the car over and parked on the side of the road. We climbed out, and Mama scanned the crowd of people for Eda. When she saw her friend surrounded by a bunch of counselors, she headed straight in her direction.

"Who's in charge around here?" Mama yelled so loudly that all these people turned around and stared at her. "Is this any way to run a summer camp?"

Eda was caught completely off guard when she first heard someone shouting—until she saw that it was Mama. Then they ran up to each other and started laughing and hugging. Everyone was watching them.

OMG—could they possibly be more embarrassing?

Eric started unpacking all the luggage from the trunk of the car. Mama and Eda came over to us, still talking and cracking jokes. They'd been friends since college, and whenever they got together, they practically acted like they were in college again, or even worse, high school.

"Love that shirt! But don't look now—I've seen at least three other people with one just like it," Mama teased her, because Eda and all the rest of the staff were wearing matching green polo shirts with the little Pine Haven emblem on them.

Eda threw up her hands in frustration. "I just bought this shirt too! How did I know it was the hottest fashion statement of the season?"

Then she put her arm around Madison. "Ah, one of my CATs! This might be your best summer ever at Pine Haven! I'm expecting you girls to be leaders. You know how all the younger campers look up to you."

Translation: Oh, Madison! Everyone wants to be you. Let me place this crown on your beautiful head so you can be Princess Perfect of Pine Haven.

"I am *so* ready for this! I've wanted to be a CAT ever since I was a little bitty Junior," Madison told her.

Molly and I were just standing there, squinting in the

sunshine. Then Eda noticed us, too. "Hi, Molly! I can tell you're excited to be here! I bet you can't wait to get down to the stables, right? And Jordan, how are you feeling, sweetheart?"

Yes, it was very important to check with the invalid and see if she was feeling okay. Was Eda waiting for green slime to shoot out of me and my head to turn backward?

"I'm great!" I said, planting a big smile on my face. "It's going to be an awesome summer!"

Mama and Eda both looked surprised by my reaction. Eda patted my back. "I'm glad to see such enthusiasm from you this year."

"Yeah, Jordan's got big plans this summer, right?" Madison smiled sweetly at me.

I tried to freeze her mouth shut with an icy glare, but it didn't work.

"Big plans?" asked Mama curiously. Even Eric peered around from the rear of the car, where he'd now piled up a small mountain of luggage in the grass beside it.

"Go ahead. Tell them what you and Molly were talking about in the car." Madison poked me with her elbow. Where was a tube of superglue when I needed it? I'd give Madison a giant spoonful, and maybe it would shut that big blabbermouth of hers for the rest of the summer.

"Jordan and I want to learn to jump this summer on horseback!" Molly blurted out.

"Hmm, I'm not sure Jordan is ready for that." Mama frowned a little.

"No, really, it was Jordan's idea. She wants to try it," Molly insisted. Was this a conspiracy? Had she and Madison planned to totally put me on the spot like this?

Then I saw Mama's face. It was lit up like a sunrise. She was *glowing*. There was really no other word for it. Instead of giving me the *Jordan, I'm so worried about you* look, she gave me something else I've hardly ever seen. The *Madison, I'm so proud of you* look.

If I had just announced that I'd discovered a cure for cancer and that I was marrying Prince William, she couldn't have been happier.

"Honey, really? You want to try jumping a horse?" Mama asked.

Now Mama, Eric, Eda, Molly, and Madison all stood around me in a semicircle. All eyes were on me. Staring. Waiting.

What else could I do?

"Yeah, I guess so," I heard myself say. "I mean, I actually want to try it. I'm going to jump a horse this summer."

CHAPTER 3

That was definitely a movie moment. There were certain moments when I felt like my life was playing out like a scene in a movie. When something really wonderful or terrible or scary would happen, it seemed like everything would freeze. And then, instead of me living my life, I would suddenly feel like I was watching my life—seeing the way it would look on a movie screen.

I hadn't meant for this to become some major announcement in front of the entire world. Already I was feeling slightly panicked. Now would probably be a good time for my liver to pop through my shirt like some alien trying to escape.

"Let's get Jordan and Molly moved in first, and then we'll take care of Madison," Mama was saying.

One good thing about Opening Day was that so much was going on, I didn't have a lot of time to worry about this now. Plus, riding lessons wouldn't start till tomorrow. That meant I could probably hold on to my various organs for the time being.

"I'm going to see if any of my friends are here yet," said Madison, scanning the crowd of people that was getting bigger by the minute.

"So—Jordan, Molly, you two are in Middler Cabin One on Side B," Eda told us, checking the list of names on her clipboard.

"Who else is in our cabin?" asked Molly.

Eda let her see the clipboard, and Molly read off the names. "Rebecca Callison and Jennifer Lawrence are on Side A. So is Melissa Bledsoe. Erin Harmon is on Side B with us, and the rest are newbies. It looks like Amber's in Cabin Two." She handed the clipboard back to Eda. "It'll be fun to have Reb and Jennifer in our cabin. The Evil Twins!"

"Twins?" Mama asked.

"They're not really twins," I told her. "They're just best friends like Molly and me. And that's just a nickname they had last year. Reb likes being the center of attention."

I was glad we were now considered old campers

instead of newbies. Pine Haven campers returned year after year, and coming here for multiple summers automatically increased your coolness level.

"I'm going to leave you all on your own for now," Eda told us. She had a lot of new arrivals to welcome. More and more cars were pulling in all the time.

Between Molly and me, we had a lot to carry—trunks, duffels, sleeping bags, pillows. It didn't help that the Middler cabins were at the very top of a huge hill in the center of camp.

Pine Haven happened to be very hilly. And there were trees everywhere. From the heart of camp, we had a great view of the Appalachian Mountains on the horizon, looking bluish gray in the sunlight.

We were partway up the hill when we heard the sound of stampeding footsteps running up behind us. "Hey, wait for us! I found your counselor!" Madison yelled.

Madison had Andrea Tisdale with her, which completely stunned me, because Tis was practically Madison's age.

Tis was the sporty-girl type, tall and lanky. She always wore her sandy blond hair in a ponytail and dressed in oversize tees with the sleeves rolled up. Hardly anybody called her by her first name. Probably most people at

Pine Haven didn't even know what it was.

"You're a counselor now?" asked Molly, adjusting the duffel bag she had on her shoulder so she could carry it more easily.

"I'm a CA this year. So I'm half a counselor," Tis said with a laugh. Counselor Assistants were the youngest counselors, seventeen or eighteen. "I'm so glad I've got Maddy Junior in my cabin!" She gave me a pat on the back.

I knew she was trying to be nice, and Tis probably already liked me for one reason: I was Madison Abernathy's little sister. But it drove me slightly insane to be called Maddy Junior. I hoped she wouldn't keep it up. Madison never got called Jordan Senior, which just goes to show how much discrimination younger siblings face.

"It's so cool we got one of Madison's friends for a counselor!" said Molly. "What's your activity? Who's the Side A counselor?"

"I'm on the tennis staff, and my co is Rachel Hoffstedder. Remember her from hiking last year? She's about five foot two, short brown hair?"

"Oh yeah, I remember Rachel," said Molly. "She's great. We've got two awesome counselors!"

"I knew Eda would make sure of that." Mama smiled

at Tis. She was overjoyed that a friend of Madison's was my counselor.

"So, Junior—you talk, right? Madison told me you're really into riding. She says you're the adventurous type, and you're gonna try some cool stunts this summer!"

I felt like hitting Madison right in the face with my pillow. She walked behind Tis and snickered evilly at me.

"Yeah, Molly and I both love horses," I said to Tis, leaving it at that.

Let's see—Madison still had to hire a skywriter to fly over camp and write in smoke letters across the sky, *My little sister is going to jump her horse this summer or else!* Then her plan would be complete.

Major, major mistake ever saying my goal out loud. Now I was starting to wish that I hadn't even told Molly about it.

We walked past the big stone building of Middler Lodge and then climbed up the steps to the long row of cabins called Middler Line. The cabins were built out of plain wooden planks, and their shiny tin roofs were blinding in the sunlight.

Since we were in Cabin 1, we didn't have far to go. Eric propped open the screen door with my overnight bag, and we carried all our luggage inside.

"All you really need is a roof over your heads, right?" said Eric. He smiled as he looked around, because there really wasn't a lot to Pine Haven's cabins. Basically, the cabin was divided into two big rooms with bunk beds and single cots lined up along the walls. No bathroom, no shower, hardly even electricity. There were a couple of lightbulbs hanging down from the wooden rafters overhead, but the only time the lights were ever on was at night. During the day, plenty of sunlight came in through the large window screens.

"Were you ever in this cabin?" Molly asked Madison. "Is your name anywhere?" She looked around at where hundreds of girls' names were written on every square inch of every wall.

"No, I was in Cabin Two and Three, so you'll find my name in those cabins in about twenty different places."

"Molly, honey, I'll help you make your bed if you find some sheets in your trunk," Mama told her.

"Okay, thanks, because I want the top bunk. Jordan will take the bottom."

Madison and Tis left us to go find some more of their friends, and once we had our beds made, Mama wanted to see if she could help Eda with anything. Eric got drafted to help other parents carry luggage to the cabins.

Molly noticed all of our name tags lying on Tis's cot,

so she pulled out hers and mine. It was kind of a pain wearing them. They were made out of a round piece of wood and lanyard string for hanging around our necks, and we had to wear them everywhere for the whole first week. But it actually was a good way to get to know everyone's name pretty fast.

Molly and I made a stop in Solitary, which was Pine Haven's name for the bathrooms. Eda had told us that even when you went to the bathroom or took a shower at Pine Haven, you probably wouldn't be alone because of the communal bathrooms, and so as a joke, they'd named them Solitary.

Then we went out on the hill to wait for our friends to get here. We found a spot in the grass and sat down, far enough away from all the arriving campers and parents so we wouldn't get trampled on.

"Hey, there's Amber!" Molly shouted when we saw a girl with long dark hair and a slightly crooked nose get out of a car. Amber was a good friend from last summer who spent all her time at the stables too. We ran over to see her.

"Did we get in the same cabin?" Amber asked excitedly when she saw us.

"No, we're in Cabin One, and you're stuck in Cabin Two with a bunch of newbies," Molly told her.

"Oh," said Amber, ultra disappointed for about ten seconds. "Well, that's okay. I'll get to meet some new people." Amber was always looking on the bright side.

We spent the rest of the morning greeting a bunch of our old friends as soon as they arrived and helping them get moved into their cabins. The charter bus pulled in just before lunch, and things really got crazy then. Counselors from Camp Crockett, the boys' camp across town, showed up to help carry luggage and get campers moved in.

Mama and Eric stayed until after lunch, but as everyone was leaving the dining hall, Mama found me in the crowd outside. "Honey, we're going to take off soon, okay?"

Now that it was time for my parents to leave, my insides got all jumpy again. And even though at my age I should have been able to do this without crying, I could still feel my eyes starting to sting a little.

"You'll be okay, won't you?" asked Mama as she hugged me really tight. Her voice had that worried sound, like she was expecting a meltdown at any minute.

"Yes!" I insisted, hoping I didn't sound too irritated. "Mama, do you remember how old Madison was the first time she jumped a horse?" I really wanted to know the answer. Plus, it distracted me from getting too emotional.

She thought for a second. "She was twelve. But Jordan, you're not Madison. You don't have to do everything just the way she did it."

"I know!" I said, and this time I really did sound annoyed. "I was just curious."

"We're going to track down Madison and say good-bye to her." Mama pointed at me. "I expect lots of letters. And I want you both to have a great summer, okay?"

"We will," I told her.

I didn't want to watch them walk away. Instead I pictured a scene in my mind. Running up to Mama on the last day of camp with a big smile on my face. "I did it! I jumped my horse, and it was awesome!" She would give me that *I'm so proud of you* look. And even Madison would have to admit, "I thought you'd wimp out, but you actually did it. Good job, Jordan."

Everyone was walking up the hill to go to the cabins, so Molly and I followed along. I had a month—one whole month. Time to turn my fantasy into reality.

CHAPTER 4

Late in the afternoon before supper, Molly and I were in the cabin unpacking. The two other girls with us on Side B were Erin Harmon and Brittany Choo.

I liked Erin, even though I didn't know her that well from last year. She had a calm, in-control kind of personality, and her gray eyes made her look like she was always thinking deep thoughts.

"So when do we start doing all the fun stuff?" asked Brittany. "Rock climbing, canoeing, tennis? Everything sounds so cool!" She pulled out a bunch of pink-striped towels from her trunk and stacked them on a shelf by her bottom bunk.

"All of the regular activities start tomorrow," Erin explained. She was sitting on her top bunk above Brittany, writing in a journal. "The first day is always crazy, with everyone getting here and finding their cabins and all the parents running around."

"I thought my parents would *never* leave!" Brittany exclaimed. "I've never been away from home for so long before, and my mom was like, 'I'm going to miss you so much,' and I'm like, 'I can't wait to get there!'" she said with a laugh. "So all three of you came here last summer?"

"Yep," said Molly.

"What kinds of insider stuff do I need to know? Or will you not tell me because I'm the new girl?" She laughed again. You couldn't help but like her. She had dark eyes and black hair, and she was cute and outgoing. She seemed to be one of those people who got along with everybody. Why were some people just born confident?

"It's a tradition that all the new campers have to make the beds for all the old campers," said Molly with a straight face.

"It is not!" I said, finally joining the conversation for the first time. I'd been trying to think of something friendly to say to Brittany from the moment we first met her, but I didn't want her to think I was pushy and weird.

On the other side of the cabin, we could hear the Side A girls and our other counselor, Rachel, still trying to decide who would get which bed. Jennifer, one half of the Evil Twins, had just arrived. She'd gotten braces since last year, and she was a lot taller, but otherwise, she was the same old Jennifer with her thick auburn hair and her slightly snobby attitude.

I could hear Jennifer trying to convince Melissa Bledsoe to switch beds with her, and even though Melissa was the quiet, mousy type, so far she hadn't given in. The other Side A girl was a newbie named Kelly, and at lunch she'd looked so stressed that she practically made *me* stressed.

Last year, since I was new, it was okay for me to be the quiet type, but now I felt like I should be all outgoing and friendly. I pictured myself saying funny things, giving directions to lost campers and parents, helping the new girls put sheets on their beds.

Instead I was sitting on my bottom bunk with a book in my lap, hidden in the shadows. The towels Brittany was sorting through had more personality than I did.

Molly pulled three books out of her trunk and looked them over. "I wonder which one I should read first." She held them up for the rest of us to see.

It was just as I figured. All three of them were about the same thing—the *Titanic*. After watching that old movie with Leonardo DiCaprio and then seeing a couple of documentaries on TV, Molly was now slightly obsessed with it.

"What does it matter? You know how it ends already," I told her.

"Very funny. This one is full of survivor accounts, this one is loaded with pictures of the ship and passengers, and this one is about exploring the wreckage. So they're all about something different." Molly raised her eyebrows at me. "What are you reading?"

"Nothing special." I was a little embarrassed letting Molly see the book I'd found in the bookstore last week. Also, I really didn't want to carry on this conversation in front of Erin and Brittany, who I barely knew.

"Hey! Why are you hiding it? Come on, let me see. Is it a mushy romance or something?" She came over to my bed and reached for the book.

"It's nothing! Here, I'll show you." I flashed the cover at her quickly.

Molly looked at the title and her forehead wrinkled. "*Our Town?* What's that about?" Erin was busy writing in her journal, and Brittany was still unpacking things and getting organized.

"It's just . . . it's a play. About people living in this small town called Grover's Corners a long time ago. You would think it's majorly boring because the people in it die of natural causes instead of drowning during a shipwreck."

Brittany laughed when she heard that. "I've heard of that play. It's kind of famous, isn't it?"

I nodded. "Yeah, I think so."

"Why are you really into plays all of a sudden?" Molly asked.

"No reason," I lied.

A couple of weeks ago, my father had taken Madison and me to see *Oliver!* performed at a youth theater. It was so amazing. There were child actors in every single role. Even the adult parts were played by teenagers. And they were just regular kids who lived in the community—not stars or anything. They didn't get paid, of course; they did it for fun because they were kids who were really into acting.

"I guess it sounds pretty interesting," said Molly, looking at the cover of my book. But I could tell she was about as interested in *Our Town* as she was in watching her toenails grow.

I was glad she hadn't asked to look at it too closely, because I'd hidden something in between the pages. A folded-up piece of blue paper. It was tucked away safe inside the book.

I flipped the pages with my thumb and caught a glimpse of the blue. I might need this paper later. Maybe. But then maybe not.

Pretty soon we heard Eda ringing the big brass bell on the dining hall porch.

"That means it's time for supper," Erin told Brittany. We left the cabin and walked down the hill with all the other campers. Even though it was only the first day, being back at camp was already starting to feel normal. That made me even more embarrassed about letting my stress levels get out of control this morning.

"Hey, there's Sarah Bergman and Whitney Carrington! Let's go say hi," said Molly. Whitney was really into horseback riding too, but Sarah was allergic to horses. Molly still couldn't get over how sad that was, but Sarah didn't seem to mind too much.

When we got close to the dining hall, I could see Madison standing in the crowd, searching around for someone. When she saw me, she headed in my direction.

"Everything going okay?" she asked, throwing one arm around my shoulder.

"Yeah, fine," I said.

"What are you mad about?" Now she grabbed me and squeezed me until my arms were squished against my chest. She always called these love hugs. I called them wrestling holds. I tried to push her away, but she had a grip like Hulk Hogan.

A couple of Senior girls walked passed us. "Oh, look! Madison's little sister looks just like her!"

"I know, right? And they're, like, so close. My sister and I fight all the time."

Maddy overheard them and grinned at me. "See what a good big sister I am? Don't you just love me?" She still hadn't let go of me, and it was hard for us to walk down a steep hill like a couple of conjoined twins.

"I love the fact that we're sleeping in separate cabins for the next month," I told her.

Then she did the most irritating thing in the world. She planted this wet, sloppy kiss on my cheek while making an ultra-loud kissing sound. She knew how I hated stuff like that.

"Ah, but I'm your guardian angel! You can never get rid of me! I'll always look out for my wittle sister!"

"Yeah, I know." That thought was slightly comforting. But also majorly annoying.

Monday, June 16

On the first real day of camp, when morning activities were about to start, everyone in our cabin was trying to figure out where to go.

"Tennis, climbing tower, canoeing, riflery." Reb read the list out loud. Last night at dinner, she'd been the last camper in our cabin to get here, and she'd come in and immediately taken charge.

"I think everyone can read," Rachel told her. Tis had already left for tennis. Last night she'd come back to the cabin long after lights out, because she'd been hanging out with all the other CAs.

"I'm only being helpful," said Reb. "I want all the new girls to feel at home." She spread her arms out wide. "Please, feel at home."

"You're so funny!" Brittany told her.

"Don't encourage her," said Rachel. You could tell Reb was the kind of camper who drove counselors crazy.

"Can you please, please hurry?" Molly was standing in the doorway, holding the screen door open for me.

I was still pulling on my riding boots.

"Finally! Now come on!"

Molly took off out the door, walking so fast I had to do a little skip to catch up with her. It was a perfect morning for riding. Overhead, the sky was a gorgeous blue, but there was still a little bit of coolness in the air. I loved how fresh the mornings in the mountains felt.

"I honestly can't wait!" Molly exclaimed, throwing her arms up in the air. "I can't believe it's been a whole year since we've seen all the Pine Haven horses!"

Molly was always excited about riding. I was just relieved that I was nice and calm, and that all my internal organs were behaving themselves at the moment.

I didn't feel at all nervous about starting lessons today. Partly because I knew we'd be reviewing things we'd already worked on.

"You think Madison will be at the stables this morning?" Molly asked.

All the CATs helped out at an activity, and since

Madison spent so much time on a horse she was practically a centaur, of course she chose riding for her activity. Why couldn't I have had a sister who was ultra talented at basket weaving?

"I'm not sure. I hope not. I don't want her hovering over me, watching every single move I make."

"Yeah, I know she gets on your nerves, but overall, she's a good sister, don't you think? Hey, there's Whitney and Amber! Let's run!"

Molly dashed off, so I raced to catch up with her. Whitney and Amber were waiting for us at the bottom of the hill. The four of us had been assigned to the same lesson time, so we were all going to be together, just like last year.

A huge smile spread across Amber's face when she saw Molly. "Wow, you look so excited!"

"Excited? You call this excited?" Molly shouted. "I wanted to sleep in the stables last night!"

"I know," agreed Whitney. "I love horses so much, I've often thought of becoming a veterinarian, but I'll do more good in the world as a doctor."

Whitney was good at lots of things. Probably her greatest talent was letting everyone know that she was good at lots of things.

The four of us walked along side by side, and we

were all dressed in shiny black boots and cream-colored riding pants. A lot of girls glanced at us as we passed the tennis courts on our way to the stables.

You didn't have to dress like this; it was fine to wear jeans and sturdy shoes for riding lessons. But I've always loved dressing up in costumes, and at this moment, it suddenly made me so happy to think that at least we all looked like expert riders. Definitely a movie moment.

"Merlin is my absolute favorite horse," said Molly. "I really hope he remembers me. I would've written him letters all winter if I thought he could understand what they were saying. When I was riding him, he seemed like he could read my mind."

"I always ride Cleo," said Whitney, pulling a scrunchie off her wrist and using it to pull back her strawberry blond hair. "Don't think I'm bragging, but of all of Pine Haven's horses, she has the best conformation."

Why would it ever cross our minds that Whitney was bragging? She tugged on her ponytail and glanced at us, waiting for us to ask what *conformation* meant. I just smiled at her and enjoyed the temporary moment of silence while her mouth was closed.

"The horse I usually ride is Caesar. I wrote a poem about him last summer, about the way he raises his head up and down when he sees me coming. It's like he's nodding hello." Amber sighed happily. "How about you, Jordan? Who's your favorite?"

"Well, last year I mostly rode Daisy." I paused, trying to think of something interesting to say about her to show that we had some ultra-psychic bond going. But I couldn't think of anything. I liked her just fine, and I got used to riding her last summer, but I'd never once thought about writing her a letter.

"She . . . she's a beautiful horse," I said finally. But it was a stupid thing to say, because she wasn't particularly beautiful. Not like Cleo—a dapple gray horse with a beautiful white mane.

Daisy was a bay. Pine Haven had lots of bays, but Cleo was one of the few gray horses. No wonder she was Whitney's favorite. But Daisy was a nice horse, and I liked her because she was really gentle.

Nobody said anything after my "beautiful" comment, and I felt like a conversation killer. Luckily, we were at the stables by now, so we all got excited again.

The stables had a big white barn with green trim on the doors and rooftop. Huge oak trees grew on either side of it, so there was always some nice shade nearby. To the right of the barn was the ring where we had our lessons, and in back was an open pasture with tall green grass growing in it.

I took a deep breath. I actually loved the way everything smelled out here. The summery smell of the hay in the horses' stalls. The rich, leathery smell of the tack, and also the scent of the saddle soap used to clean it. The smell of the horses themselves—a dusty, warm smell. And finally, the smell of manure drying in the sun. Not that I thought manure had a great smell, but when it mixed with all the other scents, it wasn't so bad.

"Hey, y'all, how's it going? My first class of the day," said Wayward, one of the riding instructors. Her real name was Caroline Heyward, but everyone called her by her nickname. Except Whitney. She always called her Caroline.

I glanced around and didn't see any sign of Madison. Good. Maybe she'd help out with the afternoon lessons. Maybe she'd never even be around at the same time I was. Maybe she couldn't even remember where the stables were.

We followed Wayward in through the wide-open stable doors. As soon as Molly saw Merlin's black face over the door of the third stall on the left, she went over to him. "Merlin! I missed you so much!" She buried her face in his neck, and he snorted at her.

Whitney made a point of going to each horse and giving it a pat. Amber went over to Caesar. He was a tobiano paint horse, mostly white with large black splotches all over. Amber murmured softly to Caesar, and he did the bobbing head thing at her.

I walked over to Daisy's stall near the end of the stable. I held my hand out for her to sniff, and her lips and tongue felt all over my open palm. Since I didn't have a treat for her, I stroked her face above her nose.

"Remember me? I used to ride you last summer." She sighed at me, and I caught a whiff of her sweet, grassy-smelling breath.

I felt bad about thinking she wasn't beautiful. Her coat was bright brown, and she was an easygoing horse who never did anything scary or unexpected when I rode her last year.

When I first started riding, I wasn't too scared about falling off, the way lots of people are. My biggest fear was that the horse would step on my foot. Every time I had to put a bridle on a horse and lead it into the ring, I'd be slightly terrified, and I'd jump if it shifted its weight a little or stamped its foot.

Right now, though, I felt perfectly relaxed. Today's lesson was going to be fun.

"Y'all want to just pet these horses, or anybody feel like having a lesson?" asked Wayward.

"We're ready! Definitely!" said Molly.

"Looks like I'm just in time," I heard a familiar voice say. I turned around to see a dark figure silhouetted in the open door.

Even though I couldn't see her face, I knew it was Madison. She stepped out of the sunlit doorway into the shadows of the stable. She was wearing riding pants and boots too, and her long dark hair was pulled back in a French braid. Everyone was always saying we looked alike, but Madison is brunette and I'm blond.

"Hey, what's up?" said Wayward. "I guess you're my assistant. Cool."

"Yep. Did Molly and Jordan tell you they want to learn to jump this summer?" Madison looked directly at me. She probably thought I'd never tell Wayward myself.

I pictured myself marching over to an already saddled horse and hopping on it. Then we'd go cantering across the pasture and jump over everything in sight— fallen logs, a stream, rail fences. That would wipe that skeptical look off Madison's face.

"Jumping, huh? That's cool. Sure, we can work up to that eventually. Not today, though." Wayward smiled slightly at Molly and me.

Wayward was the most laid-back person I'd ever met. She never wore riding breeches, just jeans, and she always had on this crazy plaid cloth hat with a little brim over her long, straight hair. She reminded me more of a skateboarder than a rider, but everyone said she'd been riding for years and that she was an amazing equestrian.

"So, Molly. I guess you'll be riding Merlin." She looked at me. "Jordan. . . ."

"I always rode Daisy last year," I reminded her.

Wayward squinted a little as she looked up and down at all the horses in their stalls. "Yeah, the thing is, I don't let Daisy jump anymore. She had an injury a few years ago."

She paused, still looking over all the horses. "Let's put you on Odie."

"I have to get used to a new horse?" I asked. My voice rose up in a really high squeak, and everyone looked at me funny.

"Don't worry. It'll be Zen," Wayward assured me.

But already my heart was pounding. A strange horse I'd never ridden before. A new skill I'd never tried before.

And jumps were dangerous. I could fall. The horse could fall. We could even fall on each other! What was I getting myself into?

CHAPTER  6

For a second I honestly felt like running to the open door at the far end of the stable and regurgitating in a pile of straw. Luckily, that feeling passed pretty quickly, but my heart wouldn't stop doing jumping jacks against my rib cage.

"Okay, y'all get your helmets on," Wayward told us.

We all went to the tack room. As soon as we stepped inside it, the rich smell of leather hit me. Saddles were lined up on several long wooden beams. Bridles, halters, bits, and other pieces of tack were hung up in neat rows all along the walls. On one side of the tack room, rows of shelves were filled with black riding helmets of different sizes.

"I don't want to switch horses! I'm used to Daisy!" I whispered to Molly.

She frowned slightly as she fastened the chin strap of her helmet. "I know, I know! But maybe you'll like Odie even better than Daisy."

"Maybe." That was a possibility. Something I hadn't even thought of. But the thing I liked about Daisy was how sweet she was. I didn't want some high-spirited stallion that would go crazy on me.

Odie turned out to be a gelding, not a stallion, but I was still slightly nervous meeting him for the first time. He was a chestnut saddlebred with a brown mane and tail, and he had a long white blaze down his face. He gazed at me with his enormous brown eyes, then snorted a few times.

I wasn't sure what he was trying to tell me. Nice to meet you? You better watch your feet or I'll step on them?

"Hi, Odie. I'm going to ride you today, okay? Take it easy on me." I stroked his neck, and he twitched his ears a little.

"Okay, everybody ready?" asked Wayward. We tightened the girth to keep the saddle from sliding while the horses walked. Now that we were about to mount, the first of my internal organs started protesting. My heart decided to go insane and started beating four times faster than normal.

Calm down, calm down, l kept thinking as we led the horses into the ring. We weren't going to jump today; we weren't even doing anything new. Why was I getting so nervous?

Before mounting, I had to tighten the girth again and adjust the stirrups, but now my fingers were starting to tremble. Madison had taken a mounting block over to Molly, since she was the shortest one in the group, and Wayward came over to me to give me a leg up. I grabbed mane and reins, stepped into her cupped hands with my left boot, and then swung my right leg over when she boosted me up.

"Feel good to be back in the saddle?" Wayward asked as I leaned over to check the girth again and adjust the stirrups.

"Yeah, it does." I tried to sound convincing. Wayward went over to help Amber. Odie must have been a few hands taller than Daisy, because I felt really high up. But he felt solid and strong underneath me. I relaxed my leg muscles and let out a slow breath.

I suddenly had a crazy thought. Maybe Odie was the horse I'd have the psychic bond with—maybe he could read my mind about jumping. Only he wouldn't get it right; he'd think I wanted to jump *right now*.

What if he took off at a gallop across the grass and went sailing over the rail fence? What if I fell and ended up with a broken neck? Look at what had happened to poor Christopher Reeve. And he'd been a really experienced rider. Everyone said it was really rare to have a serious injury like that, but was it?

What if I got my foot caught in the stirrup when I fell, and Odie dragged me for miles across rocks and rough terrain? I'd look like roadkill before Madison or Wayward could stop him! What if I fell off and he stepped on me? A thousand pounds of horse coming down on my internal organs couldn't be good for them. They'd all shoot out of me like a squished tube of toothpaste!

Odie suddenly sidestepped and raised his head with a snort. "Hey! Calm down!" I told him. I do not want to jump. I do not want to jump. Stop reading my mind! Don't you dare jump with me right now, you crazy horse!

Odie let out a high whinny that sounded like he was talking back to me. Wayward turned to look at us. "Settle down there, Ode-Man," she called to him.

My whole body felt like a rubber band that had been

twisted over and over and over again. It was either going to snap from being twisted so much, or maybe it was all going to unravel at once.

"Today, let's practice each of the gaits and let you and your horse get comfortable with each other again. We'll mostly work on walking and trotting, but we'll canter for a little bit at the end. So first the walk. Two complete circuits around, okay?" She nodded at Whitney. "Move forward to walk."

Whitney and Cleo started around the ring in a walk. After they were a few paces ahead, Amber followed them.

My heart was in serious danger of pumping overload. Was I about to be the first twelve-year-old heart attack victim?

When Amber was far enough ahead of us, I gave Odie the command. "Walk," I told him firmly, squeezing against his sides with my legs. But he wouldn't walk. He just stood still, stamping in place a little with his head raised.

"Walk, Odie!" I said, much louder, still squeezing with my legs. Behind me, I could sense Molly and Merlin waiting impatiently. Whitney and Amber were now halfway around the ring.

"Jordan, don't you know what you're doing wrong?"

asked Madison in a loud voice from where she stood across the ring, leaning against the rail fence.

"I'm using my aids, but he won't walk!" I insisted. I was really starting to dislike this horse.

"Look at your reins," Wayward reminded me in an ultra-calm voice, and then I realized I was so tense, I'd been pulling back on them the whole time.

My legs were telling him to do one thing, but my hands were giving him a completely different signal. I loosened the reins, and immediately Odie started to walk.

But the next thing I knew, Odie was out of control. He'd taken only seven or eight strides before he went straight into a trot, and suddenly we weren't way behind Amber and Whitney anymore; we were gaining on them fast!

"Hey!" was all I managed to say. I hadn't expected that transition, so I was thrown back a little, which just made me lean forward to correct so now I was bouncing around like crazy as Odie trotted briskly around the ring. Usually we'd post the trot instead of sit it, but I hadn't expected to trot at all!

Don't you dare jump over anything, you crazy nut job! I don't want to jump! I don't want to jump! Listen to me, you psycho horse!

We shot past Amber and then Whitney on the inside. Just when I thought we'd trot all the way around the ring and pass up Molly, I remembered what to do. I sank into the saddle and put tension on the reins. "Whoa!" I called. Odie finally slowed to a walk, and we came to a halt right behind Molly and Merlin.

"Um, okay," I heard Wayward saying as she walked across the ring toward me. "That was sort of unexpected." She came up and petted Odie on his shoulder. He let out a snort. "Everything all right, Jordan?"

I nodded at Wayward but kept quiet. I didn't trust my voice enough to say anything out loud. It would probably sound the way I felt—like I was about to burst into tears.

"Okay, so you know what happened, right? You transitioned from walk to trot because you were still squeezing with your legs. Odie was just doing what your aids told him to do."

"I figured that out," I managed to say in a slightly choky-sounding voice. "I'm okay now," I told her. I still couldn't believe what I'd just done.

"Yeah, Odie's a little more responsive than Daisy, so you have to be careful with your aids and make sure you're signaling what you want him to do."

"Okay." I leaned forward to stroke Odie's mane,

but my hand was shaking, so I just gripped the reins instead.

Wayward stood there beside me, patting Odie, wearing that goofy plaid hat of hers. She was so calm, which actually did make me feel better. She never got upset or annoyed or anything.

On the other side of the ring, though, I could feel Madison's eyes boring through me like laser beams. Even from this distance, I saw her disapproving look.

My face felt so hot I wanted to go stick my head in the water trough right now. So many rookie mistakes! I'd never had that many problems before. It didn't matter how understanding Wayward was about it. She was probably thinking there was no way I could work up to jumping by the end of the summer.

I'd never lost control of my horse like that. *Ever.* And in front of all my friends! I must have looked like a major greenhorn. What was my next move? Sitting backward in the saddle?

We went on with the lesson, and I tried to pay attention, but I was having trouble concentrating. Odie was a really skittish horse compared to Daisy. I could never predict when he'd toss his head unexpectedly, or side-step, or stamp his feet. The whole lesson, I never once felt like I had a good seat.

It didn't help that every five minutes, Madison would yell at me about something. "Heels down, Jordan. Relax your hands, Jordan; you're too restrictive on the reins. Jordan, bend at the hips more and keep your shoulders square."

Translation: You're not doing a single thing right. I can't believe my perfect genes are in any way related to your mutated ones.

She never once gave anyone else any "reminders." Why did she have to pick on me? Did I really look like that much of an amateur next to all my friends?

When she yelled at me to relax, saying, "You're so tense, it's upsetting your horse," I saw Wayward go over and say something to her. After that, Madison finally stopping analyzing my every move.

When the lesson ended, we dismounted and led the horses out of the ring.

Madison came over and took Odie's reins from me. "Hey, it's no big deal. You were just nervous," she said.

Oh, really? It was suddenly no big deal after she'd pointed out every single mistake I made? I didn't even bother to answer her.

As my friends and I walked back up the road into camp, they couldn't stop talking about their horses, and the lesson, and the whole summer of riding we had ahead of us, but I didn't really feel like saying anything. Nobody mentioned how ridiculous I'd looked out there, thankfully.

I was ultra relieved to say good-bye to Whitney and Amber and go back to the cabin with Molly.

I sat down on my bottom bunk and stared straight ahead. "Well, that was a disaster."

Molly was wrestling with her riding boots, trying to pull them off. "No, it wasn't a *disaster*. More than two thousand people on a sinking ship, enough lifeboats for half of them, and only seven hundred survive. *That's* a disaster."

I turned to look at her. "I could actually use a little sympathy right now. I've just had the worst riding lesson of my life. Maybe I should throw myself against an iceberg to get your attention."

Molly peeled off her sweaty socks and stuck them down inside her riding boots. She came over and sat down on the bunk next to me. "Look, I'm sorry. I know things didn't go that great today. But don't worry about it. You're still getting used to Odie. Things will go a lot better on Wednesday when we have our next lesson."

What was I thinking, telling everyone I wanted to learn to *jump*? What a joke. I'd never be able to do it. It was a fantasy to think I'd ever be the type who could try something daring and adventurous. That was Madison's role in our family. She was the adventurer.

I was the regurgitater.

"I don't even think there'll be a Wednesday lesson! I'm starting to realize I'm not very good at riding, Molly. Not like you and Amber and Whitney. I love it and everything, but I'm no good at it." My eyes were stinging, and I could already feel them starting to water.

"Oh, come on. Stop talking like that. You and I are at the exact same level. You had one bad day, that's all."

I took *Our Town* off the shelf by my bed and started randomly flipping the pages with my thumb. The folded-up piece of blue paper was still stuck inside. I hadn't showed that paper to anybody, not even Molly. At the moment, I felt like pulling it out and shredding it up into a million pieces. That was another fantasy I could never get to come true.

I stood up and walked toward the door. Fat, wet tears were rolling down my cheeks. I needed to be alone— lock myself in a bathroom stall and cry for hours.

"Jordan, wait! Don't leave. Don't get so upset about this," Molly called after me.

I pushed open the screen door and walked out. "I don't care if I never ride a horse again!"

CHAPTER 7

Wednesday, June 18

"Wow, Jordan! Your leg looks amazing," Wayward called to me from across the ring. "Feel how you're stepping down in your heel?"

I smiled back at her. We were halfway through our second lesson, and amazingly, I wasn't facing backward in the saddle, I hadn't fallen off once, and so far Odie and I hadn't gone cantering out of control across camp and ended up taking an unexpected swim in the lake. So far, anyway.

Madison had made a point of telling me every single thing I'd done wrong during the first lesson, but now Wayward was keeping an eagle eye on me to tell me all the things I was doing right.

It was working, though. I was twenty times more

relaxed today than I'd been on Monday.

"Okay, now let's work on turns," Wayward told us. We'd spent most of the lesson reviewing maneuvers like right and left turns. They were good exercises for helping us learn to coordinate using our hands and legs working together. Little by little, all my skills from last summer were coming back to me.

"Okay, nice job, Amber. Remember to keep a little more tension on your inside rein," Wayward told Amber as she made a turn.

Madison wasn't even watching our lesson today, thankfully. She was helping one of the other riding counselors, Cara Andrews, with a group of Juniors. Did Wayward plan that? Or did Cara need the extra help today? Either way, I didn't care. It made a major difference for me not to have Madison breathing down my neck.

Monday had been a slight meltdown day. I honestly thought I'd never go near the stables again after that disastrous first lesson. And it was a disaster; I didn't care what Molly had said.

Molly had left me alone for about fifteen minutes so I could go cry in Solitary, but then she'd come to the door of the bathroom stall I was hiding in and pounded on it until I'd come out.

"I'm never going back there!" I'd told her. Crying in

front of people wasn't my favorite thing in the world, but if you can't cry in front of your best friend, who can you cry in front of? "I'm going to stop taking lessons. You go without me. I'll find something else to do while you're at the stables. Like crafts."

Molly had talked to me practically nonstop that afternoon, reminding me that riding was our favorite activity, the main thing we came to camp for. "You can't give it up, Jordan. You love it too much."

"I'm obviously no good, and I will never be able to learn to jump! It's impossible! I can't do it."

Molly had practically pulled her hair out over that comment. "Nothing is impossible. Listen, after the *Titanic* sank, a bunch of men pulled themselves out of the water and climbed up on a lifeboat."

"Molly, spare me a *Titanic* story right now, please?"

"No, now listen. So anyway, it was upside down, with nobody in it, obviously. They climbed on it and balanced themselves. It was really wobbly and unstable, and there was always a chance it would tip and they'd all fall off. One of them called out directions, and they'd move a little to the left or the right when the boat shifted. It was freezing cold, it was the middle of the night, and they had to balance on this overturned lifeboat for hours."

Molly held her hands out to her sides and rocked back and forth like she was on a tightrope, showing me what the men had done.

"If the boat shifted even a little bit, they could fall in. And then they would've died. The cold water was what killed everybody, you know. Not drowning, because they were all wearing life vests. Anyway, they kept that up all night long until they were rescued the next morning. So don't tell me about impossible. Nothing's impossible."

Molly was convinced that anytime anyone needed a pep talk, there was some *Titanic* story that would work. As crazy as it sounded, her story did make me feel like I was being a little dramatic.

So I'd agreed to come back for today's lesson, even though at first I'd been really stressed.

"Ready to try left turns now?" asked Wayward. "Okay, Whitney, let's see what you got."

Amber, Molly, and I watched while Whitney made a left turn and walked toward Wayward before making another turn. The whole time she had this totally satisfied look on her face. She *was* the most advanced of all of us. She'd even done a few jumps over crossrails before.

"Most excellent!" yelled Wayward, and Whitney couldn't wipe the smug look off her face.

Now it was my turn. I wished I could tell Odie, *Just do exactly what Cleo did*. But I couldn't. I'd have to get him to make the turns myself.

I clucked at Odie, and we started forward. With my inside hand, I increased the tension on the rein while I squeezed Odie's side with my outside leg. Odie started turning left. Like magic, Odie was moving in exactly the direction I wanted him to go. Maybe he really could read my mind. "Good boy," I murmured to him softly.

When we reached Wayward, we made another left turn, and she gave me two thumbs-up. "Perfect, Jordan! Great control!" From Odie's back, I felt like I was on top of a high mountain, looking down on the beautiful world below. Definitely a movie moment.

The whole lesson was a lot of fun, and after it was over, I felt like I had progressed a major amount. I was so glad Molly had talked me into coming back today.

We all dismounted and went through the steps we needed to do for our horses. I ran up the stirrups, pulling the leather straps up so the irons wouldn't flap against Odie's sides. Then I loosened the girth and put the reins over his head so I could lead him out of the ring.

"Okay, good work today, y'all," said Wayward. "You want to keep developing your natural aids, which are . . ." She waited for us to fill in the blanks.

"Hands, legs, seat, voice," the four of us chanted together.

"Right. Your horses will do what you tell them to do, but you have to speak their language."

"Can we come back this afternoon after lessons are over and help you turn the horses out?" asked Whitney.

"Sure, we can always use extra help," Wayward said. "See ya."

As we were walking away from the stables, Molly groaned, "I'm so sore! My leg muscles are all tied up in knots." She did a couple of squats to stretch out. "Ah! This is killing me!"

"I know! I'm sore too," I agreed. The muscles in my inner thighs always hurt the worst when I hadn't been riding in a while.

"Luckily, I do gymnastics all the time, so that helps me to stay limber," said Whitney. She skipped ahead of us a few steps and did a cartwheel in the grass.

Suddenly somebody grabbed me from behind. "Hey, Babykins. How'd you do today?"

"Maddy! You scared me to death!" I yelled. She'd come up behind me, and now she had me in one of her boa constrictor hugs. And why'd she have to call me by that stupid nickname?

"So? How'd your lesson go?"

"Everything went really well. *Today*," I said. She was leaning against my back like she was about to hop on for a piggyback ride. "You're squishing me, by the way."

"Hey, I saw you making those turns. Looking good, Jordan. Your problem on Monday was you were so nervous, you were freaking Odie out. Horses are really sensitive. A nervous rider equals a nervous horse."

"Yeah, that was one of my problems," I said, wriggling free of her arms at last.

"Oh, you mean *I* was your problem? I'm just trying to help you. I want you to do your best."

I was secretly glad that Madison had seen me during my lesson. I did look good today. I really could ride well under the right conditions.

"I know! Now can we leave? We're late for . . . tennis." Actually, we had no plans to go to tennis. I just wanted to get away before Madison did anything else to me—called me another nickname, started giving me tennis advice, or crushed me in a sumo hold.

"I just wanted to say you did a good job today. Keep it up and you'll definitely be ready for crossrails by the end of the summer."

"Thanks for the vote of confidence," I said, in what was only a slightly snotty voice.

The four of us walked down the long dirt road away

from the stables. When we were far enough away, Molly poked me in the side with her elbow. "You're so mean to Madison. She's just trying to look out for you."

"I am not!" I protested. "I can't believe you called me mean." I crossed my arms and walked ahead of her along the shady road.

"Okay, not mean, I guess. It's just so obvious you want her to leave you alone."

"That's because I do want her to leave me alone!"

"Just be glad you have a sister. You could be an only child like me," said Whitney. "I would *love* to have Madison for a big sister. She's so pretty, and she's popular and outgoing. Don't you just love her?"

"Yeah, all the CATs are cool, but Madison's, like, everybody's favorite," Amber gushed. "You're lucky, Jordan. I bet my older brother hasn't even noticed I'm at camp right now. Madison's really nice."

"Yes, you're all right. Let's see—Madison's nice, pretty, popular, outgoing . . ." I counted off all her many qualities on my fingers. "Next time I see her, I'll crown her Princess Perfect."

Molly and Amber laughed out loud over that, but Whitney just shook her head and frowned at how ungrateful I was to have such an amazing sister.

Of course I loved Madison. She was my sister. It's

practically a law that you have to love the people in your family. But didn't they all see how much pressure she'd put me under the other day? Sure, she was trying to help me. She would love it if I turned out to be a Madison clone.

I'd be so happy if I could learn to jump this summer. But was that enough?

Even if I did jump, I could already hear what people would say. *Oh, look at Maddy Junior! She's just like her big sister!*

But Madison and I weren't anything alike. Maybe we looked alike, but the similarities stopped there. I could never be like Madison—confident, adventurous, daring. That just wasn't me.

No matter how good I got at riding, I'd just be Madison's little sister. What would it be like if I did something that was all my own—just me?

CHAPTER 8

Friday, June 20

"I'm glad the rain finally stopped," said Maggie, a girl from Cabin 4. "I hate rainy days at camp."

We had just walked into the lodge for evening program, and the noise of all the Middlers crammed into one space was a little deafening. The lodge was one big room with high ceilings and wooden rafters overhead, and tonight there was a fire going in the fireplace, since the rain this afternoon had made everything damp and chilly.

"Really? I happen to like rainy days." We found a spot on the floor where we could sit down near Melissa, Brittany, and Erin.

"Well, at least we didn't miss our riding lesson because of the rain," Molly said.

I thought the rainy afternoon had been a lot of fun. After lunch, we'd gone back down to the stables to watch a group of Senior girls do a jump course. We'd all run to the stables for cover when the rain came, and the smell of the rain, the horses, the hay, and the leather had all mixed together.

"Erin and I were at the climbing tower, so a bunch of us ended up on the dining hall porch. I like rainy days too," said Brittany.

The counselors had been out on the porch of the lodge, planning something for tonight, but then they all filed in through the doors.

Libby Sheppard, one of the swimming counselors, announced, "Tonight we bring to you a skit performed by your exceptionally talented counselors! Presenting a fractured fairy tale for your enjoyment—here's the story of 'Prissyrella'!"

We did lots of different things at evening program— games and contests and things like that, but skits were my favorite. I loved watching all the counselors perform.

Then Michelle Burns, a counselor from Cabin 2, came out wearing a "wig" that looked like she'd stolen it from a mop. She held up a mirror and brushed her stringy gray mop hair and sighed, "Pine Haven is *soooo* boring with no boys around! I can't wait till the first dance with Camp Crockett."

Next, a bunch of counselors told Prissyrella she couldn't go to the dance until she went to all the great activities available at Pine Haven. So Prissyrella had to swim a lap across the lake, climb to the top of the climbing tower, and hit a bull's-eye in riflery before she could go to the dance.

All during the skit, the counselors were obviously loving being onstage and drawing attention to themselves. I wondered if maybe some of them were a little bit nervous performing in front of all of us. Did they think they looked stupid? Were they at all self-conscious? They definitely didn't show it if they were.

Our two counselors were really fighting for the spotlight. Tis kept intentionally scooting in front of Rachel since Rachel was so short, but Rachel would grab Tis around the waist and drag her off the stage, then run back to her former spot. They had the whole lodge in hysterics over their competition for center stage.

If only I could be like that. If only I could be on a stage and not care about how I looked or what people thought about me.

It was so not me to act that way. But wasn't that why they called it acting? Because you weren't on stage being yourself. You were pretending to be someone else. And why couldn't you pretend to be someone who was confident and outgoing? It was like stepping outside of yourself and becoming someone new, at least for a little while. What would that be like?

At the end of the skit, Prissyrella decided she'd rather go on a hiking overnight than go to the Camp Crockett dance. "I can have so much more fun at Pine Haven doing all the activities I love!" Prissyrella announced at the end.

"What a shameless plug for all the camp activities," Reb muttered from where she was sitting on a bench with Kelly and Jennifer.

"Maybe that means we're having a dance tomorrow night!" Jennifer suggested.

"Maybe that means they've canceled the dance and we're all going on an overnight!" said Reb, which made Jennifer really mad.

While we were all talking and laughing, the counselors tried to get our attention again. "So you've just seen our version of one fractured fairy tale, 'Prissyrella.' Now it's your turn. Every cabin needs to come up with your own fractured fairy tale and perform a skit for the rest of us," announced Libby Sheppard.

All over the lodge, you could hear everyone groaning.

Most people thought it was fun to watch the counselors do skits, but they hated it when they'd make us do them too.

"What if we can't think of anything?" asked JD Duckworth, a loud girl from Cabin 2.

"What if we have no talent?" asked Reb.

"You're all very talented, and you'll be able to think of something if you work together. So everybody, go to your cabins, make your plans, and meet back here in half an hour," Libby told everyone.

"Half an hour?" Molly asked. "That's impossible. We can't come up with an idea in half an hour." We were starting to file out through the big double doors.

Actually, I loved this idea. I thought it would be majorly fun to plan a skit for the whole cabin to perform.

"Sure we can," I said. "We just have to get creative. With eight people, we can come up with something really good."

It still smelled rainy, and we could hear drops of water falling off the leaves of the trees. We jumped over puddles as we climbed the stone steps toward Middler Line. "Which fairy tale should we do?" I asked everyone. I already had one idea, but I didn't want to be one of those bossy people who takes over.

Ahead of us in the crowd, Whitney was already telling her cabin what to do. "We should do Snow White and the Seven Dwarves, because we have exactly eight people. I'll be Snow White, because probably the rest of you want to be dwarves."

Translation: I want the starring role for myself.

"I know I've dreamed my whole life of being a dwarf," I heard Whitney's best friend Sarah say. She happened to be the tallest girl in their cabin.

"I got a great idea! Let's do Snow White and the Seven Dwarfs!" Reb shouted. Whitney turned and glared at her, and Reb gave her a friendly wave.

The hardest part about planning a skit with a group of eight people was not coming up with ideas. It was trying to get everyone involved. As soon as we got to the cabin, the Side A girls went right over to their side and plopped down on their bunks.

"Okay, somebody think of something," Reb ordered. She stretched out on her bed and closed her eyes. Kelly and Jennifer weren't any help either. And forget Melissa. She would hardly say anything.

At the beginning of the week, Kelly had gone to all the activities with Melissa, but the last couple of days, it seemed like she'd dumped her for Reb and Jennifer instead.

"Well, here's an idea," I said. "And we don't have to do it. If somebody else can think of something better, we should definitely do that."

Everybody looked at me, and I felt really embarrassed. "What about Little Red Riding Hood?" I said, in a voice that was suddenly all hoarse and congested.

I cleared my throat. "Except instead of it being a wolf that Little Red Riding Hood goes to see, we could make it Eda. We could do an impersonation of her. You know, like, 'Let's hear some of that Pine Haven spirit!'" I said, doing my best Eda voice, which I happened to think was pretty good.

Everybody stared at me without saying a word. It was a horrible idea. I should've kept my mouth closed.

Then everyone laughed. "You sound just like her!" said Molly.

"You even looked like her for a second!" agreed Brittany.

"That's a great idea. What else?" asked Erin.

I couldn't keep from smiling. "Well, let's see. We could do something like . . . Little Green Pine Haven Camper." It sounded stupid the moment I said it.

"Perfect," said Reb. "Okay, Jordan, tell us what to do and we'll do it."

And just like that, I was suddenly in charge of the

whole skit. I've never been in charge of anything before. I'm not a take-charge kind of person. But everyone else was so majorly bored with the idea of having to plan a skit and so happy to let me do it all, that I did. The ideas were pouring out of me.

"So Little Green Pine Haven Camper thinks she's going to visit her counselor," I said, sort of thinking out loud.

"Her sick counselor?" asked Molly.

"Uh, no. Her counselor's . . . exhausted. Because she just got back late from raiding the kitchen," I said. "In fact, Eda is mad at all the counselors for raiding the kitchen every night."

"Which is true!" said Brittany. "And so Eda fires all the counselors, and she's hiding in bed when Little Green Pine Haven Camper comes to visit. Does she have enormous teeth?"

"No, an enormous clipboard," I blurted out, because Eda never went anywhere without her clipboard. I was shocked when everyone roared with laughter over that.

"Good one, Jordan! 'My, what an enormous clipboard you have!'" said Reb. "I'm starting to see this."

"What can we use for a clipboard?" asked Molly.

After looking around the cabin, we eventually figured out something that would work. Molly pulled out this kind of cardboard thingy in her duffel that was supposed to make the bottom of it lay flat, and if you carried it under your arm, it actually did look sort of like an enormous clipboard.

I was thinking about how Eda always wore skirts—white skirts, denim skirts, khaki skirts. They were short and casual, but it would be funny to spoof that in some way. "Besides her enormous teeth, Little Green Pine Haven Camper is also amazed by Eda's stylish skirts," I said.

"Oh my gosh! That's a great idea! Hang on one second!" Brittany ran over to Side B and then came back holding up a silvery, metallic-looking skirt. "It can be this!"

"Where did you get that? Do you actually wear that?" asked Molly with her mouth hanging open.

Brittany laughed. "I haven't yet! My mom thought it was cute. She said I could wear it to the dance. I'm like, 'Why don't you just buy me a roll of aluminum foil?'"

Jennifer shook her head in disbelief. "You could be struck by lightning in that thing."

"It's perfect," I agreed. "And Eda wears Pine Haven polos a lot, so maybe we could do something like . . . 'What a strange green shirt you're wearing.'"

I paused for a second. "I got it! You know how

Wayward never wears the official Pine Haven polo? She always wears that green T-shirt with a snowboarder on it that says, 'What day is it, anyway?' Maybe we could borrow that!"

"Oh, that is too funny!" shouted Molly.

Jennifer, Reb, and Kelly were all laughing too. "Now we just need to figure out who's going to play which part," said Reb. "Okay, Jordan, what's it going to be?"

I was so excited that everyone else was finally getting into the spirit of doing this. Molly went to find Wayward to borrow her shirt. The rest of us started planning out the whole skit, coming up with lines, figuring out props, and deciding who would play what.

And I was basically the one in charge. Everyone was listening to me, and asking me to make decisions, and expecting me to plan everything out. That was really surprising and weird, but at the same time, I loved it.

So I decided that at the beginning of the skit, the counselors, played by Molly, Jennifer, and Kelly, would all be raiding the kitchen. Then Eda, played by Reb, would come in wearing her shiny skirt and Wayward's T-shirt, carrying her enormous clipboard. Once she'd fired all the counselors, she would crawl into a sleeping bag to take a nap, and that's when Little Green Pine Haven Camper would come in.

I picked Brittany to play the part of the camper, because she could act all sweet and innocent easily. Erin would be the narrator. Melissa said she didn't want a part.

"I don't want one either," I said.

"No way, you have to be in it. You should play Eda," said Reb. "You're the one who can do the best imitation of her."

"Yeah! Do it, Jordan! Do that same voice you did a minute ago," said Brittany.

I could do it. I could be Eda. I could put on the costume and carry the big clipboard and do my impersonation. Instead of just doing it in front of a few people, I could do it in front of everyone.

I could see the scene in my mind. Me walking into the lodge dressed as Eda, so sure of myself. Delivering lines and getting laughs. What would that be like?

But then, all of a sudden, my stomach muscles felt like a clenched fist. Was I ready for this? What if I got up there and felt like regurgitating instead of saying my lines?

"I'm the director, and the director never plays a part," I told them all. As soon as I said that, my stomach muscles relaxed.

Melissa glanced at me and gave me a little smile. I

could tell she didn't want to stand up in front of everyone either.

"That's not true," said Kelly. "Lots of directors make appearances in their movies. Like Hitchcock. He showed up in all his movies."

"Well, I'm not going to!" I insisted, slightly yelling. "I just don't want to, okay? I planned everything, so if I don't want a part, you can't make me!"

Reb held her hands up. "Chill! We're not going to force you to do it. Give me that piece of aluminum foil, and I'll be Eda."

I did feel better, knowing I wasn't going to have to get up in front of everyone.

Once we had everything planned out, we went back down to the lodge. One by one, each cabin performed their fractured fairy tale. Cabin 3's version of Snow White was actually pretty good, even if Whitney did overact. Everyone in Cabin 4 acted bored doing Goldilocks and the Three Bears. They'd probably put about five minutes of preparation into it.

When it was our cabin's turn, just seeing all my cabinmates up there in front of everyone made me nervous for them. My heart pounded so loud I could hardly hear some of the lines, and I had to keep my hands folded in my lap because they were trembling.

I had no idea why watching everyone else made me so uptight, but it did. Maybe because the skit was mostly my idea.

But it was incredible. When Reb walked in with her costume, carrying that oversize "clipboard," the whole lodge went insane, and the audience laughed for practically five whole minutes. Everyone remembered their lines, we got tons and tons of laughs, and at the end, the applause almost made me deaf. The counselors especially loved our skit.

"I wish Eda could have seen that," said Libby Sheppard. She smiled at all of Cabin 1's actors.

It was definitely a movie moment. And I was really okay with the fact that no one realized I'd been the one who'd planned the whole thing. The main thing was that we'd done a great skit. I should be happy about that.

When evening program ended, we got in the goodnight circle and sang "Taps," then had graham crackers and milk before going back to the cabin to get ready for bed.

As Molly was climbing up to her top bunk, she stopped and looked at me. "You should've been Eda. Reb got lots of laughs, but she made Eda sound like a little old lady. Your impersonation was much better."

As soon as Molly said that, I felt a sad, heavy lump

in my stomach. I knew she was right. I could've done a better job.

But at least Reb had the guts to get up in front of everyone. She didn't sit in the audience with her hands folded, trying to keep them from shaking.

"Thanks, but I had enough fun just planning it," I said. My voice actually sounded slightly convincing.

Everyone was changing and getting ready for bed. Tis was asking us all where Kelly, Reb, and Jennifer were because they weren't in the cabin, but then they showed up, looking like they'd been up to something.

I crawled into my bottom bunk and pulled the covers up around me. I couldn't stop thinking about how the whole skit had gone.

I'd planned everything. At least that was something. I'd just panicked at the thought of actually being in the skit. But I could've done it. Maybe I would've been nervous. Maybe I wouldn't have been able to say all my lines very well.

But then, who knows? Maybe everything would've gone just fine. Maybe I would've even been good at it.

It was almost time for lights out, but I took *Our Town* off my shelf. I flipped to the middle of the book where the blue piece of paper was hidden inside.

I took it out and looked at it. It was folded into

quarters. The whole time I'd been at camp, I hadn't once unfolded it to look at what it said. I didn't need to. I'd read this piece of paper so many times, I had all the words memorized.

Why did I even pick up this paper in the first place? Was I ever going to need it? Probably not.

I started to unfold the paper to read it one more time. But then I stopped myself. Instead of reading it, I stuck the paper back inside my book before I put it away on the shelf.

Saturday, June 21

"Are you excited about seeing your boyfriend?" Molly asked me, raising her voice so I could hear her over the sound of the music playing in the background.

"He is not my boyfriend!" I snapped, but that only made her laugh.

We had just walked inside Camp Crockett's dining hall for the first dance of the summer. It was a major deal. We'd all spent the whole afternoon waiting in long lines for the showers, racing around trying to find hair dryers, borrowing clothes from each other, and getting dressed in something besides the T-shirts and shorts we'd been wearing all week. Everyone always went slightly crazy on the day of a dance. And now here we all were.

The Camp Crockett boys were crammed together

on one side of the dining hall, and all of us Pine Haven girls were in a huge cluster by the doors. So far the two separate groups hadn't blended together at all.

Molly had been teasing me all day about seeing Ethan Hurley again. Last summer, we'd danced together at both dances.

He'd even written me. Twice. Once at camp, between the first and second dance. And then about a week after camp ended, he'd sent me an e-mail. I e-mailed him back, but then he never replied. So of course I couldn't write him again either.

Even though I kept acting to Molly like it was no big deal, I'd still been thinking about Ethan all day. What would our reunion be like after not seeing each other for a whole year?

Reunions were always movie moments. We'd be standing in the dining hall with crowds of people all around us, and there'd be lots of noise from the music. But the whole time, I'd be looking at all the faces in the crowd, trying to see *his* face.

That's when I would see him. He'd be looking around, straining to see over all the people in the crowd. Then his eyes would meet mine, and his face would break into a smile. I would smile back, but there would still be about a hundred people between us.

With a frustrated look, Ethan would glance at the crowd in his way. We would both be pushing through the hordes of people, but it would take us a long time to get through them. The whole time, we'd keep our eyes on each other—until finally we'd meet in the middle.

"Hi, Jordan. I was hoping I'd see you here."

"Hi, Ethan. I was looking for you, too."

I kept telling Molly there was a good chance Ethan didn't even come back to Camp Crockett this year. But I couldn't stop looking through the crowd of boys for him. He had blond hair, and he was on the short side, about Molly's height. But he was really cute, and we'd had a good time last year at both dances.

"There's a good chance he did come back," Molly was saying.

"Maybe. Maybe not," I told her.

"No, I see him. He's wearing a green shirt."

Ethan was talking to two other boys in the crowd. His hair was a lot longer now. It actually looked really good on him. Suddenly the thought of carrying on a conversation with him made my whole face blush. So I spun around and took off in the opposite direction. Had he seen me?

"Hey! Where are you going? Aren't you going to talk to him?" asked Molly, following after me.

Now the big open space in the middle of the dining room was filling up with people dancing. The music was turned up high, and I could feel the vibrations of it as I weaved in and out of all the people clustered together.

"I can't just walk up to him and start talking to him. What would I say?"

"Good question. Why don't you go crazy on him and say something like 'Hi.' Then if you really want to walk on the wild side, you could say, 'How are you doing?'"

"Shut up. I slightly hate you for making fun of me right now."

"I can't believe this! You know the guy. You've danced with him. You've written him letters. Why are you suddenly terrified about talking to him now?"

I finally stopped walking because I felt like we were deep enough in the crowd that he couldn't see me anymore. "I'm not terrified. I'm just not sure he wants to talk to me."

Molly clutched her head in her hands and groaned out loud. "Why wouldn't he want to talk to you?"

I grabbed her by the arm and pulled her closer. "Maybe he doesn't like me anymore," I said. "Why did he never write me back after I wrote him?"

Molly sighed. "He probably just got busy. Don't take it personally."

"But what if I said something stupid in my e-mail? What if he wants to avoid seeing me tonight?" I said. I was trying to keep my voice down, but it was hard to carry on a conversation with loud music blaring all around us.

"Why don't you go stand out in plain sight," she suggested. "Then, if he doesn't come talk to you, you'll know he doesn't like you. If he does, then you can stop acting like a slice of fruitcake."

We were in the middle of this conversation, so I didn't see him approaching me. Not Ethan. Another boy with short red hair and braces. "Uh, hi. Do you want to dance?" He was looking directly at me, so he obviously didn't mean Molly.

He caught me so completely off guard that all I could do was stand there with my mouth open.

I didn't want to say yes. Ethan might see me dancing with him, and then he'd leave me alone for the rest of the night. But I didn't want to hurt this boy's feelings. What could I possibly say to get out of dancing with him?

"My shoes hurt my feet," I blurted out finally. "They're giving me blisters."

Molly swiveled her head around and gave me the strangest look. "On your brain, maybe." Then she looked at the guy. "My friend has to go soak her feet, but I'll dance with you." She walked away with the red-headed boy, and the two of them were laughing by the time they were out on the dance floor.

I couldn't believe she'd said that! If I was going to soak anything at the moment, it would be my flaming hot face. In the punch bowl.

So now here I was, standing all by myself looking lonely and abandoned. What if Ethan saw me right now? What would he think? I glanced around quickly, and luckily, I saw Whitney a few feet away. For whatever reason, she wasn't with her best friend Sarah at the moment. I rushed over to her.

"Hi, Whitney. Mind if I hang out with you while Molly dances?"

Translation: Don't you dare leave me standing here all alone, or I'll have to hide under a chair.

"Hi, Jordan. I love that outfit."

I glanced down at my cropped pink jeans and pink-and-white-striped shirt. I wasn't sure—had I overdosed on pink tonight? Did I look like a bottle of Pepto-Bismol?

"Thanks," I said, feeling a lot pinker than I wanted to feel at the moment.

After Molly had danced with the redheaded boy, she

found Whitney and me. Luckily, she kept her mouth shut about Ethan until Whitney got asked to dance. When the two of us were alone again, she demanded, "Why haven't you talked to Ethan yet?"

"Because I'm waiting for him to come over and say hi to me first."

"Why does he have to say hi first? This *is* the twenty-first century, you know. Girls don't have to sit around waiting for boys to come to them. We can make the first move."

"I don't want to stalk him! Boys hate that."

"Jordan, so far you haven't gotten within five hundred feet of him or even made eye contact. I'm pretty sure that stalkers tend to be a wee bit more outgoing than that. What's the worst thing that could happen if you said hi to him?"

I could think of about fifteen bad things that might happen. Number one, he didn't remember me. Number two, he didn't like me anymore because of some random, weird thing I'd said in that e-mail last year. Number three, he had a girlfriend back home. Number four, he had his eye on someone else he wanted to dance with. Number five, he was looking at me right now and thinking, *What did I ever see in that pink nightmare?*

But if I tried to explain this to Molly, she'd tell me

I was just making excuses. "So you're saying you'd be willing to go up to any boy here and ask him to dance?" I asked her.

"Sure I would. Why not? What's the worst thing he could do?"

"Laugh in your face. Say no. Make up some lame excuse why he doesn't want to dance with you."

"Oh, like, 'Sorry I can't dance with you. I have blisters on my brain'?" asked Molly.

"Just because I didn't run right over to him the second I saw him and say, 'I can see my future, and guess what—you're in it,' doesn't mean I won't talk to him eventually," I told her.

Molly put one hand on my shoulder. "Look, I know you're afraid. But sometimes you have to face your fears. You know what would've happened to you if you'd been on the *Titanic*?"

I glared at her. "Are you going to tell me I would've drowned?"

"Yes! And you know why? Because you're afraid. A lot of people were afraid to get in the lifeboats at first. They didn't want to be lowered hundreds of feet into the cold, dark ocean. They wanted to stay on that warm, safe, *unsinkable* ship. You wouldn't have gotten on a lifeboat, Jordan. But I would have! Don't you get it?"

"No, I don't. What's your point?" I asked. I was totally confused by how lifeboats applied to me talking to Ethan.

"My point is, sometimes you have to face your fears and do something that looks dangerous. It just might save your life." Molly crossed her arms and nodded at me, convinced that she'd just given me an amazing argument.

"Well, you're wrong about me drowning on the *Titanic*. I would've been too afraid to cross the ocean on a ship in the first place. So fear can save your life."

Molly sighed. "I give up. I'm going to ask that boy to dance with me. The band kept playing till the end, Jordan. Right up until the ship sank. Remember that!"

Okay, I had no idea what that was supposed to mean, but I didn't want her abandoning me again.

"Molly, wait!" I yelled. But she'd already walked over and asked a tall, skinny boy in a "Rock Star" T-shirt to dance with her. How could she leave me alone like this?

Just then I felt someone's hands on my shoulders. A really deep voice said, "Hey, cutie. Wanna dance?"

CHAPTER 10

I almost died. It honestly felt like my heart dropped out of my chest—not a healthy situation at all. I also completely stopped breathing, and that's not particularly good for long-term survival either. The hands swiveled me around, and I was facing—Rob Thompson.

"Rob! You scared me to death!" I hissed at him through clenched teeth. Rob was Eda's son. He was a Camp Crockett counselor. He was nineteen and more than six feet tall, so he towered over me like a tree.

Rob laughed at my reaction. He was the closest thing Madison and I had to a big brother. He teased both of us a lot, but me especially, since I'm so much younger than he is.

Rob's sandy blond curls were cut short to keep them

from completely taking over his head, which curly hair can do very easily if you don't watch it. He wore glasses and had a little bit of acne, but otherwise, he was sort of cute, in a slightly geeky way.

"Hey, small stuff—you're not dancing. The question is why. Insecurities? Lack of rhythm? Bunions?"

I frowned at him. "I have danced. A little," I lied. I was pretty sure Rob hadn't watched me every single second, so how would he know the difference?

"Oh, yeah?" His eyebrows went up above the rims of his glasses. "Listen. I've personally seen at least two different guys walk up to you. You either turn them down or walk away. That is *cold*, my little sista. Icy. Frosty. Glacial. You can't be dissing these little dudes like that. You'll give them a complex. Break their hearts. Crush their souls."

"Why don't you go embarrass Madison now, okay, please? That is, if you can find her. She's dressed like a shrub."

Madison and all the other CATs were busy doing Porch Patrol duty. That meant they walked around outside Camp Crockett's dining hall with flashlights to make sure nobody went past the dining hall porch. They always made it a big deal by dressing up in camouflage and taping tree branches and leaves to their clothes.

"Uh, yeah, nice try to get rid of me. I've seen her already. I actually saved her from a vicious woodpecker attack. Certain death loomed before her, had I not been there with my swift reflexes. So now you're my next project." Rob propped his elbow on my shoulder and leaned down.

"Okay, small stuff. Look around. These are the finest that Camp Crockett has to offer, I'm sorry to say. Pathetic. Disappointing. Downright sad. But you're only twelve, so it's not like you've got lofty standards—am I right?"

"I wish I was invisible," I groaned. Why was Rob torturing me like this?

"Eh, sorry. Can't help you there. My invisibility cloak's at the cleaner's. Here's what I want you to do." He was still leaning on me. "Name the little dude of your dreams. Point him out. He's yours. Done deal. I'll work my magic, and you'll be paired with him for the rest of this romantic evening."

I covered my face with my hands. "This is the worst night of my life." I ducked out from under Rob's elbow and tried to walk away, but he blocked my escape.

"Jordan. Seriously. You ought to dance. Are you sure you don't want me to fix you up with someone? How about one of the little dudes in my cabin?"

At that moment, I happened to see something that made my heart feel like it really had fallen out of my chest. And then someone had stepped on it. It was now all covered in dust, lying flattened under everyone's feet.

Because I looked across the dance floor and saw that Ethan was now dancing with Kelly.

So much for waiting until he came to me. I'd been right all along. He didn't want to talk to me again. He didn't like me anymore. He'd had his eye on someone else instead.

"What's up?" Rob asked me, looking across the dining hall to see what it was I was suddenly so focused on.

"Nothing. I just want to hang out with my friends tonight, okay?"

Rob put his hand on my head before walking away. "Okay. See you later. Maybe I will go bother Madison."

I buried myself in the crowd so Ethan wouldn't see me. Eventually Molly found me, and I told her what had happened. From where we were standing, I could see Kelly talking to Ethan at the refreshment table. Now Reb was over there too with the boy she'd been dancing with. My whole night was over.

"You should've listened to me! He probably gave up because he thought you were trying to avoid him!"

"Why would he think that?" I asked her in disbelief.

"Because, Jordan, I saw him try to walk up to you a couple of times, but you'd always run away!"

"I wasn't trying to avoid him! I was just . . . embarrassed."

"You know that, and I know that, but how would he know that? Anyway, never mind. I'll ask a boy for you. Just point out someone you like," Molly told me.

Why did everyone always think they had to help me get a boy to dance with me? Was I that pathetic?

"No!" I yelled.

"Fine. But you could still have fun if you'd just dance a few times at least."

The rest of the night was majorly horrible. Even though I tried not to, I couldn't keep from watching Kelly and Ethan together. I'd always liked Kelly, and she had no way of knowing that Ethan and I knew each other from last year. But that didn't make it any easier to see the two of them talking and smiling.

A couple of times, it looked like a boy was about to ask me to dance. But I would walk away before he could get too close. I just wasn't in the mood anymore. I knew I wouldn't be any fun tonight.

When the dance was over, I was ultra depressed. We left Camp Crockett's dining hall and went outside to get into the vans and trucks that would take us back to Pine Haven. Molly and I barely talked at all.

But once we got back to camp, we were walking up the hill together in the dark. "I have to talk to you about something," she said suddenly.

"If you tell me another *Titanic* story, I'm going to jump overboard without a life vest," I warned her.

"Okay, I won't. But I do want to say something to you."

I sighed out loud. "Go ahead."

"I just want to say this. I know you get scared sometimes, Jordan. Everybody does. But you let it get to you too much."

I didn't say anything. Kelly, Reb, and Jennifer were walking up the hill ahead of us, laughing and talking. They'd all had a great night.

"Look, I can understand you being afraid about learning to jump. You could fall off. You could get hurt. That makes sense. And you know, last night when we were doing the skit and you backed out of it? I can understand that, too. Lots of people are afraid of getting up in front of a group. I was a little nervous doing the skit too."

I tried to look at her, but I couldn't see her face in the dark. "You were?"

"Yeah, I was. But I did it. And I really, really wish you'd done it. Because you would've been good at it."

"Thanks," I said. I was really wishing now that I'd done it too.

"Anyway, I can understand you being afraid of stuff like that. But what happened to you tonight? You made talking to Ethan this huge, huge deal. And it wasn't. You really wimped out. And it's your own fault you didn't dance one single time tonight."

"Oh, thank you so much. This makes me feel so much better, hearing this from my *best friend*."

"Yeah, I am your best friend. Which is why I have to be the one to tell you this. You let your fear get to you sometimes, Jordan. You blow things up in your mind and make them a lot worse than they really are. Sometimes you just have to face your fears."

"Oh, really?" I said, ultra sarcastically. It was a stupid thing to say, but I couldn't think of anything else.

"You know I'm right," said Molly.

I refused to answer her. Because she *was* right.

I did make talking to Ethan a really big deal. I did imagine one disaster after another. Why could I always picture the worst-case scenario happening, but I could never believe that there might sometimes be a best-case scenario?

What if I'd done my Eda impersonation last night and everyone had loved it?

What if I'd gone to say hello to Ethan and he'd been happy to see me and we'd danced together all night?

I looked up at the stars. I picked out the brightest one I saw and made a wish. Just once I'd like to be brave. Just once I'd like to do something without being scared. Just once—just one time—I wish I could be fearless.

CHAPTER 11

Monday, June 23

Up, down, up, down, up, down, up, down. Trotting had a real rhythm to it—a two-beat count that you could feel. Odie and I trotted around the ring, and I rose up and down in the saddle in what felt like perfect sync with his movements. The sound of his hooves pounding against the dirt sort of hypnotized me.

After a week of lessons, Odie and I were really getting used to each other now. He didn't act all out of control and unpredictable anymore, now that I'd calmed down a lot. And it sort of made me laugh to remember how freaked out I'd been last week, thinking that he would decide to jump on his own.

"Looking good, Jordan," commented Wayward as Odie and I passed her in the ring.

"Thanks," I said. It came out sounding breathless, because posting the trot was a pretty good workout.

The four of us were spread out evenly, trotting around the ring. Whitney looked great when she was posting. Although I hated to admit it, her posture really was close to perfect. Bent at the hips, shoulders back. Rising up out of the saddle, but not too far, and then coming back down in a smooth motion without plopping down on Cleo's back.

Amber looked pretty good too, but I noticed her shoulders were hunched forward, and she was pulling back on her reins too much. Molly tended to rise up way too high when she posted. It was sort of funny to watch, because she'd practically be standing in the stirrups on the upbeat. Wayward kept reminding her, "Not too high."

"Okay, now let's work on sitting the trot. You know this is a lot bumpier, so start off at a slower pace."

"So why are you sometimes supposed to post and sometimes not?" asked Molly.

"It's good to practice sitting the trot. It helps you learn to balance and absorb shock in the right places. You need good balance to jump, right?"

"Right!" said Molly.

So then we trotted around the ring several more

times. Sitting did take some getting used to. Once you'd gotten the hang of posting, you'd kind of naturally rise up out of the saddle. It was way bumpier sitting the whole time, and as we sped up, a couple of times I felt like I'd be bounced right off. I could feel myself getting tenser the faster we went around the ring.

"Ease up on the reins, Jordan," Wayward reminded me. I liked how calm her voice sounded. It was nice these days not to have Madison helping out with every single lesson, analyzing everything I did wrong. Wayward seemed to know just what to do with me. She'd give me compliments when I needed them, but when I was doing something wrong, she'd be very mellow about telling me how to fix it. I liked that about her.

"Looking good!" Wayward called to all of us. "One last thing I want to work on. Go one whole time around the ring in two-point."

Two-point position meant we had to rise up out of the saddle and bend forward at the hips. We wouldn't post, we wouldn't sit; we'd just stay in that position the whole time. It looked similar to the position that jockeys rode in, and it was tough on abs and leg muscles. Plus, it was a lot of work just keeping balanced in that position for a long time.

"I know I'm working you hard today, but you'll love me later," Wayward called to us.

I could hear Amber groaning a little. Molly was doing a great job. Whitney did it the best. Big surprise there. She probably loved being the top student in the class.

"Okay, let's stop there," Wayward announced, and I sat back down in the saddle, so relieved I could finally relax my muscles.

I leaned forward and gave Odie a pat. "Good boy," I told him, stroking his brown mane.

There were times when I still missed Daisy a little. She had such a sweet personality. But I was definitely getting to know Odie. Like whenever I murmured to him, he'd nicker back at me softly like he was trying to talk to me. And anytime we were standing still during our lesson, maybe to take turns doing an exercise or to listen to new instructions from Wayward, he'd turn his head a little to look over his shoulder at me.

It was like he was checking, "Are you still back there?" I'd give him a pat, and then he'd turn around again. I liked that about him. I always felt like he was thinking, *Just making sure you're still in the saddle.*

For the last couple of lessons, Wayward had let Whitney do a few jumps over the crossrail, and so now

Molly, Amber, and I kept our horses standing in the center of the ring so we could watch Whitney.

The crossrail Whitney was about to jump was set up at the end of the ring. There were two poles crossed over each other to form an X shape with standards on each end to hold them up. You were supposed to get your horse to jump in the center where the poles crossed together, because that was the lowest point.

"That looks so easy!" said Molly. "I bet we could jump that today, no problem at all."

"It does look pretty basic," I agreed. When I saw what our first jump actually looked like, I was ultra relieved because it was so low.

It was just like Molly had said. I did tend to blow things up and make them a lot worse than they really were. In my mind, I'd made jumping to be this really scary and dangerous thing. Whenever I pictured myself doing it, I always imagined my horse and me jumping over a brick wall. A really high brick wall.

Now I realized how ridiculous that was. Maybe someday, years from now, I might be able to jump over a wall, but that wasn't the way they started off beginners.

"Yeah, it looks easy, but you have to do everything right," Amber reminded us. "You have to stay in two-point and make sure you're stepping down in your heel so your leg doesn't slide back. And you have to jump the center of the crossrail and ride on a straight line the whole time!"

We watched Whitney make her approach. She had Cleo in a trot, and as they got close to the crossrail, she got into two-point position. Then, just like that, Cleo jumped over with no effort at all.

"See! It's simple! Nothing to it," insisted Molly. "I wish Wayward would let me try that now. I think I'm ready for it."

"Well, maybe not today. But we'll be doing it soon," I told her.

Whitney rode back over to where the rest of us were waiting, and we all dismounted and led our horses out of the ring.

"Looks like Madison is keeping busy with the Juniors," said Molly. We could see Madison helping Cara Andrews with her beginner class. She noticed us watching and gave us a quick wave, but she was too busy and too far away to come over and talk to us. I didn't mind *seeing* Madison at all my lessons. I just didn't want to have to *hear* her.

I liked the long walk back to camp, because the road was quiet and deserted. Nobody ever came down it unless they were going to or from the stables. A soft breeze rustled the leaves of the tree branches stretching over our heads, and the sound of our boots kicking up the dust of the road had a steady beat to it.

"You make jumping look so easy," I told Whitney.

Whitney's head was already swollen over how good she was at everything. Giving her a compliment might turn her into a human bobble-head, but she did look like a natural out there.

"Thank you. I appreciate that." She often talked like that—really stiff and formal.

"Were you scared the first time you jumped?" I asked her.

"Not really. Jumping over low crossrails is actually quite an easy way to start out." Whitney glanced at me. "Try not to let it scare you. Once you do it, you'll feel so much better."

I smiled back at her. "I think you're right."

Just as we were passing Crafts Cabin, we saw Eda out on the porch with a few Junior girls. She had her video camera, and she was filming them as they made placemats out of strips of cloth. When she noticed us walking up the road from the stables, she waved good-bye to the little girls and came over to talk to us.

"Hi, ladies. Did you all have a good time at the stables today?"

"It was awesome!" said Molly. "We're getting better with every lesson."

"But we're sore!" said Amber. "We've all got achy muscles from riding all week."

"Oh, Madison, I got an e-mail from your mom today," Eda said, looking right at me.

That happened a lot. Just about everyone at some point would get mixed up and call me Madison. Even Mama did it. There were probably times when she called Madison Jordan, but somehow I never seemed to hear that.

I smiled at Eda, because what else could I do? "Oh, really? What did she say?" I asked, trying to sound polite.

"Oh, she was just wondering how your riding lessons were going. She said she'd gotten one letter from you last week, but you hadn't mentioned riding at all."

Translation: Your mother expects me to spy on you all summer. So were you serious about learning to jump, or was that just a bunch of hoo-ha to impress us?

"Oh. They're going really well. Just like Molly said. Today we did a lot of trot work. And Wayward has us practicing two-point so we can be ready to jump in a couple of weeks."

That was what she wanted to hear, right? I could just

imagine what else Mama must have said in her e-mail.

Has she thrown up lately? Has she thrown up on any of the horses? Will she ever turn out to be anything like Madison, my perfect firstborn nonregurgitater?

Eda smiled happily at me and gave me a one-armed hug. "Great! Why don't you write her and tell her all that? She'll be so happy to hear about it."

"I will. Definitely," I said.

"Hey, could you videotape us when we're ready to jump?" asked Molly. "That way, our parents could see the tape later and they wouldn't just have to hear about it."

"Of course! Anytime," Eda told her.

"My parents would love that," said Amber.

"That really is a good idea," said Whitney. "Seeing ourselves jump would be a good way for us to improve our form."

"Great! Let me know when you're ready, and I'll come down with the camera." Eda said good-bye to us and headed off in the direction of the office.

"Oh, that's going to be so cool! We'll have a video-tape of us jumping!" said Molly.

I pictured my videotape. I'd be on the back of Odie, and I'd approach the jump just like Whitney had done. I'd be in two-point, bent at the hips, shoulders squared, eyes focused straight ahead. I wouldn't be worried about any of the things that could go wrong. I'd be fearless.

He'd take off at just the right moment, and together the two of us would fly over the crossrail exactly in the center.

That's what I wanted my video to look like. And maybe it would. Maybe my first jump would be the best movie moment of my life.

But how could I be sure it really would look like that? Real life wasn't always like the movies. And sometimes you couldn't do a retake.

CHAPTER 12

Tuesday, June 24

"Okay, Jordan. What should we do? You plan every-thing, and we'll do it," said Reb. She was lying on her cot, propped up on one elbow. She looked at me, wait-ing to see what I'd come up with this time.

"Yeah! You're really good at this stuff, Jordan," Brittany added from where she sat on Jennifer's trunk. "Our cabin had probably the best fractured fairy tale, don't you think?"

We were all crowded around on Side A, trying to plan tonight's skit. Molly and I were sitting on Rachel's bed, and everyone was staring at me.

At the start of evening program, the counselors had done a short skit for us where they pretended to be campers. They complained about having to be quiet during rest hour, having to be quiet after lights out, and having to clean up the cabins for morning inspection. They made it funny and everything, but basically, they made us out to be a bunch of whining complainers.

At the end of the skit, Jamie Young, a CA who was best friends with Tis, announced, "You've seen our imitation of you. Now you get to imitate us! Take half an hour to plan a skit. Then come back and perform it for us. So be creative, be funny, but don't be too harsh on us!"

So here we were, all eight of us, trying to come up with some ideas of how we were going to imitate Rachel and Tis. And all eyes were on me.

"Well, I think Molly would make a good Rachel, because they sort of look alike," I said. They were both short, and they had dark brown hair. "And then for Tis, maybe Reb could play that part."

Reb seemed like a good choice because they were both sporty girls with blond hair. But that wasn't the only reason. Both of them were very sure of themselves.

I paused to see if anyone would disagree, but everyone just nodded and waited for me to go on.

"So I was thinking we should do something about Tis and Rachel that only we know about. Because we're the ones who actually live with them." I smiled slightly, because I knew exactly what I wanted to do. "What about the way Rachel talks in her sleep?"

"Yeah, but she never really says anything. She just mumbles," said Kelly.

"Well, you know how Rachel loves to sing all the camp songs, but she's always off-key? Why don't we have her singing camp songs in her sleep?"

Erin nodded. "Good idea. Yeah, that would be funny. But what about Tis?"

"What about the way Tis kisses her tennis racket?" I suggested.

The whole cabin exploded when I said that. I couldn't believe how hard everyone was laughing. I sat there with a smile on my face and waited for them to get quiet again.

Tis had this really expensive tennis racket that she said had taken her six months to save up for before she could afford it. She had a funny habit of giving it a little kiss on the strings before she'd hang it up on a nail over her bed at the end of the day.

"Oh my gosh! Tis is going to die when she sees this!" said Brittany.

"It'll be great, though! Let's do that," said Molly. She ran to our side of the cabin and got Tis's tennis racket off the nail to give to Reb.

Reb took the racket from her and held it up, frowning a little. "Flat face; long, skinny neck. He's not really my type."

"We don't care! You have to kiss it!" Brittany told her.

So Reb clutched the racket in her arms and planted six or seven kisses on the strings.

"Everyone else can be campers," I suggested, "and you'll all be reacting to the singing and the racket kissing."

"But let's all be in the skit this time," said Erin, looking right at Melissa and me. "Nobody can say, 'I don't want a part.' There'll be three Side A campers having to listen to Rachel sing and three Side B campers watching Tis kiss her racket."

Melissa and I exchanged quick looks. "Okay," I agreed.

I really did want to be in the skit, even though I knew I'd be nervous. But I'd made up my mind. No more wimping out. Time to be fearless.

I came up with some funny lines for all of us campers to deliver, and after that, we rehearsed everything a couple of times to be sure we had it all down.

Then it was time for us all to meet back in the lodge. All the Middlers were crowding inside and finding seats on the wooden benches or the floor. Our cabin sat together as a group.

"We'll go first!" Reb announced loudly when the counselors all came in.

Tis saw that Reb was holding her tennis racket. "You better be careful with that! If I see one scratch on it . . ."

"I'll treat it with tender loving care," Reb said, as we all stood up and made our way to the front of the crowd.

At least we weren't on an actual stage—just some empty floor space at the front of the lodge where no one was sitting. It seemed less intimidating this way.

Even so, I broke out into a cold sweat the second I turned around and was facing all the other Middlers. Luckily, Brittany, Erin, and I were supposed to be sitting on the floor playing cards for our part in the scene, so I felt much better when we sat down. This way I could be sure that my knees wouldn't buckle underneath me.

Brittany dealt the cards, and I clutched mine with my sweaty hands. Could everyone in the front rows see that my cards were shaking? I tried to hold my hands still. The skit had started, and everyone was delivering their lines, but I could hardly concentrate on what anyone was saying.

All I could think of was the fact that I'd have to

deliver my one and only line soon. What if when I said my line, it came out all croaky sounding? Or what if I messed up the words? Or didn't say it loud enough? Why did I even give myself a line in the first place?

Molly was getting a lot of laughs every time she sang in her sleep. But Reb was about to bring the lodge down with her racket kissing. So far everything was going great. But I still didn't dare take my eyes off my cards. Was anyone looking at me? Did my face look as tense as it felt? Hopefully, they were all focused on Reb and Molly.

My line was about to come up. Should I clear my throat now? Or would that make too much noise?

"I'm really worried about her," said Erin, which was the cue for my line.

I glanced at Reb and opened my mouth, hoping my voice would come out sounding normal. "It could be worse. At least she's not an archery counselor."

"You're right," said Brittany. "She'd get pierced lips from kissing the arrows." That line got a big laugh, just like I hoped it would.

Whew! I was done, done, done! I'd said my one line, and I hadn't choked! And Brittany had gotten a good laugh. My shoulders relaxed a little, and I could feel my heartbeat slowly returning to normal.

I could've given myself the funny line, but I figured Brittany would do a better job of it. And she had. It had been great.

After the skit was over, everyone applauded, and Reb stepped forward to take a bow. That made the rest of us line up and do the same thing.

"Way to go, Cabin One!" JD Duckworth yelled.

"That was a good one," I heard Boo Bauer say.

We sat down in the crowd, and I felt weak from being so tense through the whole thing. But I was also so, so relieved.

And happy! I'd done it! I didn't back out! I'd actually gotten up and taken at least a small role in our skit.

We watched the rest of the cabins perform their counselor imitations, and lots of them were really good. I just loved seeing all my friends perform and have a fun time.

Later that night after evening program was over, we were all walking up the steps to the cabin together when Reb made this announcement: "From now on, whenever we have to do any kind of skit, let's just put Jordan in charge."

"Yeah, good idea," agreed Jennifer. "Skits, the talent show, all that stuff. It's good to have at least one person in the cabin to take care of all that."

The talent show! I hadn't even thought about that. Every summer the whole camp would have a talent show, and each cabin had to do at least one act. It could be anything—singing, dancing, playing a musical instrument. Or doing some kind of skit.

"Okay," I said. "I promise I'll plan things, but you'll all have to be in it."

I couldn't believe it! It was so cool that everyone thought of me as the one to plan these things. But there was something else I was thinking about.

I could hardly wait to get back to the cabin. As soon as I crawled into bed, I pulled *Our Town* off my shelf and flipped through the pages until I came to the blue sheet hidden inside. For the first time in weeks, I wanted to read the words printed on this piece of paper. I unfolded it and spread out the wrinkles.

WANT TO BE A PART OF VALLEY
YOUTH THEATER?
AUDITION FOR OUR NEXT PLAY!

WHAT: Our Town
WHEN: Auditions held from 6 to 8 p.m.,
August 1 and 2

WHO: All aspiring actors between the
ages of 9 and 17
HOW: Bring headshot (school photo
okay) and your best acting chops
WHERE: Valley Youth Theater,
708 S. 3rd St.
See you then . . . and break a leg!

I'd first picked up this paper back when I'd gone with
Daddy and Madison to see *Oliver!* No one knew about it
and what it made me think of doing.

Something daring. Something unexpected.

Something fearless.

CHAPTER 13

Friday, June 27

Late in the afternoon, after all the lessons were over, we were on our way back to the stables to help the riding staff hose down the horses, feed them, and turn them out. Amber and Molly really loved doing this, because the more time they got to spend with the horses, the happier they were.

Whitney liked to do it because she thought it somehow gave her more status than the other riders who only took lessons and didn't help with tacking and grooming.

I liked it at first, but after doing it a few times, it seemed like a lot of work to me. But all my friends wanted to do it practically every day, so I figured I might as well go along with them.

When we got to the stables, we could see that Madison was out in the ring riding Suzy. We walked over and stood beside Wayward, who was leaning against the rail fence, watching them.

"Hey, how's it going? We'll start hosing down the horses in a minute, after Maddy finishes this course," Wayward told us.

I actually liked watching Princess Perfect on horseback. Madison looked like she belonged on a horse, and it made me proud that all my friends got to see her too.

"Suzy is so beautiful. I love white horses," said Molly. She reached up to try to steal Wayward's plaid cap, but she wasn't fast enough. Wayward kept both hands on her hat so Molly couldn't get it.

"Don't mess with the hat," she warned. "And Suzy's not really white. She's gray." Then Wayward explained that white horses were really rare. For a horse to be called white, it had to have pink skin. Suzy's gray coat had faded to white as she'd gotten older.

I didn't really care whether Suzy was technically white or not. She *looked* white to me. And with Madison riding her, the two of them looked beautiful together. They were pretty far away from us, but they stood out against the deep green of the grass.

Madison was wearing a red polo, cream-colored

jodhpurs, and black boots. Her brown hair was flow-ing out from under her riding helmet in a loose pony-tail that hung down her back. And when she broke into a canter, her hair flew up in the air.

"Oh, wow! We get to watch Madison practice jumps," said Amber.

"Yeah, since we keep her busy helping out with lessons, she doesn't get a lot of time to ride," said Wayward.

The jump course set up in the ring had some verti-cals, some hay bales, and an oxer, which was two rails with a space in between for the horse to jump at one time.

Wayward explained to Madison how she should complete the course. "Pick up your canter and take the red and white vertical, then turn left over the blue oxer and ride straight ahead to the hay bales. Remember to keep her balanced."

"That's a very advanced course, isn't it, Caroline?" asked Whitney. Whenever she called Wayward by her real name, I'd sometimes forget who she was talking to.

"Yep, pretty advanced. Y'all will work up to that someday," she told us with a wink.

The sun was really low in the sky now, and Madison and Suzy were bathed in yellowy sunlight. Madison was cantering around the ring, and we watched as she took the first jump over the vertical. Then she had to make a quick turn to the inside and loop back around to the oxer. They sprung over it so gracefully I could feel myself smiling as I watched them.

Madison did get on my nerves at times. Sometimes a lot. But she was still my sister.

"Wow, she is so *good,*" marveled Amber.

"She's better than good," I said. "She's awesome." I had to shade my eyes with one hand so I could see her in the setting sunlight, but what I saw made my heart feel like a huge balloon swelling up with helium.

When they cantered past us, I could see the look of concentration in her eyes, but that wasn't the only thing. I could see in her face how much she loved being on the back of a horse, how completely and totally happy she was, how perfect this moment was for her.

If this were a movie, there would've been a close-up of Madison's face right now with the golden sunlight making her look like she was glowing. And there would be beautiful music playing in the background.

Maddy had finished the whole course and was going back around to do it one more time. When she got to the third jump, the hay bales, she and Suzy flew over those and went straight to the vertical.

But something didn't look right. Madison's reins had gotten a little long and suddenly Suzy's head went down. Madison was thrown forward and . . .

"She fell!" Wayward said. Her voice hit me like an electric shock.

Suzy's hooves came down on the poles, and Madison . . . Madison was on the ground!

"Oh my gosh!" yelled Amber.

Wayward was over the rail fence in one leap, and the rest of us scrambled over behind her.

We ran as fast as we could across the field. My whole body jarred as I ran. Everything was a blur of green. The world rushed past me in crazy, tilted camera angles. The sound of all of us running, running, running was so loud I could feel the ground shaking.

Maddy, Maddy!

What if she was . . . ? Or even worse! What if she was . . . ? I couldn't even think those words!

No, no! Please, God, make her okay! Make her okay!

Now I could see her, lying there in the grass, on one side, her body curled up. One arm was thrown back behind her in an awkward, twisted way. But then she sat up, slowly.

Not dead! Not paralyzed!

Now she was standing. A little wobbly. Her back to us, bending over. She took off her helmet, and her hair was all messed up.

Wayward got to her first. "Are you okay?" she shouted.

Me still running, like in a dream, when you run and run and run and run, but you don't get anywhere.

I could see her. Standing. Nodding. Still bent over, her back to us. Hands on her knees. Like she was searching for something she'd dropped in the grass.

After two years of running, I finally got to her. But when she turned around . . .

Her face . . .

Blood! Blood everywhere!

Gushing from her nose, her mouth! Blood covering her face! Her beautiful face!

"Mah," I managed to say before the ground rose up and knocked me down.

CHAPTER 14

"Jordan. Jordan." Someone was calling my name, but they were underwater.

Or I was underwater.

"Um," I said because I knew I should try to answer them.

"Can you open your eyes?"

Maybe. Later.

"Jordan, can you hear me?"

"Um."

And then it felt like an elephant was sitting on my chest. I sucked in my breath all at once. I must've forgotten to breathe for a second. My eyelids fluttered open. A circle of heads was leaning over me.

Then I remembered. Maddy!

I screamed and covered my eyes. Maddy hurt! Bleeding!

"Holy guacamole, what a scream." That was Wayward. I'd recognize that voice anywhere. She still sounded *so calm*.

"Ow, that hurt my ears." I couldn't tell whose voice that was.

"Hey, Jordan. Are you okay?"

I opened my eyes, and Molly and Amber were bending over me. Molly's dark eyes stared down at me. "I think she's okay. Right, Jordan?"

I nodded. My head felt like a horse had stepped on it. Suzy was standing a few feet away with her head hanging down.

Did Suzy step on my head? Was that why I was on the ground?

"Maddy? Where's Maddy?" I asked, whimpering a little bit.

"She's over there. Wayward's taking care of her. She just has a bloody nose, that's all. And Suzy's okay too. She just feels bad about Maddy falling," said Amber.

Now Whitney was looking down at me. "I got the first aid kit. I ran straight to the tack room for it because I figured we would need it. You shouldn't try to move. You may even be in shock."

"Yeah, wow! I've never seen anybody faint before," Molly said. I could tell how impressed she was by the sound of her voice. "You just fell right over. Like a tree. One minute you were on your feet, and then *bam!* Right over!"

Hearing Molly say that made my legs feel weak and trembly. The memory of what it had felt like washed over me. Like getting hit by a wave in the ocean. Except it was the ground that had knocked me down.

"Is Maddy okay? Is she hurt?" I asked.

"She's fine. Really. It looked bad, but it was just a bloody nose," Amber said, squatting down over me. "Are you sure you're okay? You scared us to death!"

"Yeah, I think so." Prickly blades of grass poked into my bare arms. I sat up slowly. I still felt a little dizzy and disoriented. A few feet away from us, Wayward was bending over Madison.

Maddy was sitting in the grass, holding a wad of gauze up to her nose. On her cheek was a streak of dried blood, but other than that, she looked slightly normal.

But the second I saw her I started crying, and I couldn't stop. I leaned forward and rested my arms and head on my bent knees, so at least everybody couldn't see my face. Someone sat down in the grass beside me and started rubbing my back.

I knew it was Maddy. I could tell by the smell of her shampoo. "I'm fine, Babykins. I just got a nosebleed. I didn't mean to scare you so bad. And then you scared us."

I turned my head to the side and peeked at her out of one eye. "Are you sure you're okay? There was blood everywhere!"

She pressed the wad of bloody gauze against her nose. "Yeah, I know. It must've looked pretty grisly. But really—I'm okay. I just bumped my nose into the back of Suzy's neck when I fell off. Good thing my shirt's red, huh?" She ran her hand across the front of her red polo, and I could see that there was a darker red stain all across it.

"What happened?" I asked, still in this choky, crying voice. "Why did you fall?"

"Well, between the hay bales and the vertical, Suzy should've taken it in two canter strides, but she did it in one. As soon as she started the takeoff, I knew we were too far away from the jump."

"Yeah, I saw that too, and I thought, 'Uh-oh, not good,'" said Wayward. She was checking Suzy over and patting her shoulder. "You're okay, aren't you, girl? No swelling. No sign of injuries."

Madison smiled at me. "See, I'm fine; Suzy's fine. It's no big deal. I've fallen lots of times before." She was still rubbing my back in a circular motion. It reminded me of the way Mama used to rub my back when I was little and she was trying to get me to fall asleep.

I'd never fainted before. Ever. I still felt very weak and shaky.

"I think you both need to see a doctor, just to make sure everything's okay," said Whitney. "If you want, I'll run back to camp and alert Eda."

"Nah, they don't need a doctor. But maybe you should both go see the nurse. Tell her what happened and she'll probably give you a popsicle," said Wayward. "Was that wild, or what? Bloody nose, fainting. Intense! Everything's Zen now, though."

I couldn't believe what Madison had just said.

I turned and looked at her. "Really? You've fallen lots of times?" Madison was such a good rider. I'd never even heard about her falling off *once,* much less *lots of times.* Why was I just now hearing about this?

You'd think that kind of thing might come up at the dinner table. Oh, by the way, I fell off my horse today and almost broke my nose.

"Just about everybody falls at some point. I usually just get up and brush myself off."

"You mean when you're jumping? That's when you've fallen?" I asked. Did Mama know about this?

"Yeah, sometimes. But I've fallen when I was cantering, too." She looked up at Wayward. "How many times have you fallen off a horse?"

Wayward shook her head. "Too many to count."

"Why do we do this if someone could get hurt?" I suddenly yelled.

Madison shushed me. "Calm down. No one's going to get hurt."

"You just did! You're covered in blood!" I was practically screaming now.

"But I'm fine. I'm not really *that* hurt," Madison tried to assure me.

I knew people took falls on horseback. That was something I'd sort of always known about in the back of my mind. But so far I'd never fallen.

So far.

But Madison and Wayward fell? Too many times to count? They were good riders. Experienced riders.

Why were we involved in such a dangerous sport?

Was it really worth it if someone could get hurt?

CHAPTER 15

Monday, June 30

"How much does a horse cost?" asked Molly.

"Thousands of dollars," said Whitney.

"Really? That much? I guess I can't talk my parents into that," Molly said with a sigh. The four of us were walking along the shady road on our way to the stables, and everyone was in a great mood, as always.

Except for me.

It was the first time we'd been back to the stables since Maddy had taken that fall, and the last thing I wanted to do today was get on a horse.

"Do you live out in the country with lots of land?" asked Amber. She pulled her long dark hair back and wrapped an elastic around it.

"No, just the suburbs," Molly said. She was kicking

a rock with the toe of her boot as we walked down the dirt road. Her mouth twisted into a slight frown. "Someday, maybe. When I'm grown up and I have a job, the first thing I'll buy is a horse."

"The first thing you should buy is some land to put the horse on," said Whitney in a bossy voice.

"You okay, Jordan?" asked Amber.

"Yeah, fine." I nodded, but I didn't feel fine.

I was beginning to think that I was having what people call a panic attack. I honestly felt like I was going to crack, like an eggshell, and then crumble into a million pieces.

The closer we got to the stables, the worse I felt. I tried to put it out of my mind, but I kept seeing that horrible vision.

Maddy's face covered in blood.

She's fine, she's fine, she's fine, she's fine.

Once she'd gotten all the blood washed off her face, she looked perfectly normal. And except for a couple of bumps and bruises, she really wasn't hurt at all.

So why wouldn't my brain believe that? Why did it keep showing me that picture of her bloody face in my head?

Talk about a movie moment. I was definitely having one right now, but it was a scene from a horror movie.

Stop it. I'm not going to think about that! Kittens. A field of daisies. Fluffy white clouds.

I tried to get a different picture stuck in my brain, but I knew that for the rest of my life, I'd remember the way Madison looked when she turned around that day with all that blood pouring out of her nose.

"Boarding a horse? You mean like the horse doesn't live with you?" Molly was saying.

"Yes, maybe you live in town, but there might be someone who lives out in the country. So you pay that person to let you keep your horse in their barn."

"Wow, I didn't know you could do that! Maybe I could talk my parents into that!"

By now we had made it to the stables. But I felt like all the bones in my body had turned to limp spaghetti noodles. That's how wobbly I felt.

All of a sudden, a thought popped into my head. *Whatever you do, do not get on a horse today.*

Maybe this was a sign, a warning of some kind.

Molly had told me that a lot of people had had psychic warnings about the *Titanic.* There was one woman who had a really bad feeling as soon as she was on board. She refused to go to sleep at night because she had this feeling that whatever bad thing was going to happen would come during the night. As soon as she felt the ship bump against the iceberg that night, she knew it was the horrible thing she'd been dreading. She and her daughter managed to escape on a lifeboat, but her husband went down with the ship.

I stopped in my tracks and sank down into a squat, right there in front of the stables.

"Jordan! Are you okay?" Amber gasped. She rushed over to me and bent down in front of me. "What's wrong?"

I couldn't tell her that I'd just hit an iceberg.

"I . . . I feel a little dizzy," I said. Now Molly and Whitney were standing over me too.

"Are you going to faint again?" asked Whitney. "Maybe you should lie down. I'll run back into camp and get the nurse."

She was just about to take off when I stopped her. "Whitney, come back. I'm not going to faint." I sat down in the grass under one of the shady oak trees and rested my head on my bent knees.

It was slightly embarrassing to have everybody think I was about to faint again. I didn't feel like that, but I did feel majorly freaked out over the thought of getting on a horse right now.

My heart sort of felt like it was fluttering around

like a butterfly. My breathing was really fast, almost like I was panting. I tried to force myself to take slow, deep breaths.

Wayward was standing in the open doorway of the stable when she looked out and saw us. "Hey, what's up? Everything all right over there?" she called to us.

"Jordan's going to faint!" yelled Whitney.

"I am not!" I shouted. "I just feel a little weird."

All three of my friends stood around in a circle, hovering over me. Wayward came walking over. "Not feeling so good?"

"Just a little dizzy," I said. "Don't worry about me. You all go ahead and start the lesson. I'm just going to sit here for a few minutes until I feel better."

"Are you sure you're okay?" Wayward asked. "You need anything? Some water? Anything?"

"No, I'm okay," I assured them. "I'll be fine. You just go ahead."

They looked at me for a few long seconds before they slowly walked away. "Let us know if you need anything," Wayward said again.

"I will," I said, and now my voice sounded almost cheerful.

The one good thing about fainting was that now

people were afraid I'd do it again. They didn't want to push me. I could tell they were all a little worried that if I stood up, I'd keel right over.

I waited until they had all disappeared into the stable, and then I stood up. I started walking slowly down the road. Once I was far enough away and no one could see me, I walked even faster. I walked back up the long road toward camp all by myself. I couldn't believe how much better I suddenly felt.

Back on Middler Line, all the cabins were deserted, since morning activities had started. I went inside our empty cabin and took off my riding boots, changed out of my riding pants into a pair of shorts, and then stretched out on my bottom bunk.

I took *Our Town* off the shelf by my bed and spent the rest of the activity period reading it. It was great. The cabin all to myself, no riding lesson, no one to pressure me, nothing that I had to do. It felt like getting an unexpected day off from school.

Why was I so glad to get out of the riding lesson?

Because they were a lot of work. I was always really tired after they were over. And lots of times during the lesson, I'd be so worried about keeping my heels down and my back straight and gripping with my legs but not squeezing and all the other dozens of things I had to remember that I hardly ever just had fun.

Riding could be fun at times, and I did like the horses and all that, but lately, I was beginning to wonder. Molly, Whitney, and Amber talked about horses 24/7, but sometimes I didn't even pay attention to what they were saying.

I mean, I was getting used to Odie, and I liked him, but it wasn't going to break my heart to say good-bye to him when camp was over. I just didn't have the bond with him that everyone else seemed to have with their horses. Why was that?

Maybe I just wasn't that into it.

Reb, Jennifer, and Kelly came back to the cabin to change into swimsuits and then left again. The next time the screen door opened, Molly walked in. Her short brown hair was all sweaty and stuck against her forehead from wearing a riding helmet.

"Hey, how are you feeling?" Her boots made a loud clomping sound as she walked across the wooden floor.

"Better," I said, sitting up on my bunk.

Molly sat down on top of her trunk to pull off her boots.

"You didn't really feel like you were going to faint, did you?" she asked, giving me a really direct look.

I shrugged. "Not really. But I *was* feeling weird. Not

like I was going to faint. Just . . . all jittery inside."

Molly pulled off her socks and dropped them on the floor beside her bare feet. "Jordan, I know what's going on. You're letting yourself get freaked out over what happened to Madison the other day. Don't you know what people say? If you fall off a horse, you have to get right back on it."

"But *I* didn't fall off a horse. And Madison *did* get right back on it."

Molly squinted at me suspiciously. "So you mean you'll go to the next lesson and you'll be fine? You won't act like you're about to faint or make up some excuse?"

I clutched *Our Town* and sat up on the edge of my cot. "There's something I want to tell you."

Suddenly I wanted to let Molly in on my secret. I felt like I had to tell her right this second.

She pushed her sweaty bangs out of her eyes. "You look really serious. What is it?"

"It's a secret. A major, major secret," I said, still gripping my book in one hand. "Promise me you won't tell anyone."

"Wow. Okay. I promise I won't tell anyone." She came over and sat down next to me on my bottom bunk. "Now I'm dying to hear this."

I flipped nervously through *Our Town* for the blue paper. When I found it, I took it out and handed it to her.

She had a curious look on her face as she unfolded it, and I watched as her eyes scanned the page. She glanced up at me with a blank expression.

I took a deep breath and said the words I'd been thinking in my head for more than a month now.

"I'm thinking about trying out for this play."

Molly's eyes bulged like a cartoon character's. "Seriously?" was all she could say.

I nodded. "Seriously. You know how much I love doing skits and stuff. And everyone said they wanted me to think of something for our cabin to do for the talent show. All of that's good practice, right?"

"Yeah, I guess so." She sounded surprised. "I didn't realize you were that into acting, though."

"Molly, this is all I think about. I want to audition for this play. I think this is something I really want to do."

"So that's why you're reading that weird book!"

"It's not a weird book. And yes, that's why I'm reading it." Then I told Molly the story about how Daddy, Madison, and I had gone to see *Oliver!* and how exciting it had been to watch all the actors in the youth theater perform onstage.

"I sat there and watched them, and all I could think about was how cool it all was. Did you even know there were theaters like this where the whole cast is made up of kids? It's kind of like a school play, because anyone who wants to can try out. I couldn't believe it when I saw these announcements lying on a table. I took one and folded it up and stuck it inside my purse."

I jumped up from my bunk. I was pacing up and down the floor, walking and talking really fast.

"Then I went home and looked at their website. I found out all kinds of stuff there. First you audition, and then if you make it, they have rehearsals for a few weeks. After that, they do the shows on the weekends for a whole month! And once that show is over, you can try out again for the next one! I just love this idea!"

"It sounds really cool," Molly said, watching me walk back and forth.

"But Molly, I'm so terrified! I want to do it, but I don't want to do it. Does that make any sense?"

"Yeah, it does. It's exactly the way you feel about learning to jump. You want to do it, but at the same time, it scares you."

I went over and sat down beside her on my bed. "What would you say if I told you I'd changed my mind?"

Molly stared up at the ceiling. "You're really unpre-dictable. Ten seconds ago you said you wanted to try out for this play. Now you've already changed your mind?"

I took a deep breath and prepared for the hurricane that I knew was about to hit. "I don't mean the play. I mean I've changed my mind about learning to jump. I don't want to do it anymore. And don't bother trying to talk me into it."

I might as well have told Molly that I was staying on the *Titanic* and there was no way she'd ever get me in a lifeboat.

"Jordan! You have to jump! You have to! We're so close! It's not even going to be that hard!"

"I know. It probably won't be that hard, but I don't want to do it now."

"But you told everyone you were going to do it! Your parents, Eda, Madison, Wayward. Everyone's expecting you to do it. I thought you wanted to show everyone that you could do this." Molly grabbed the pillow from my bed and punched it with her fist.

"Well, I did. But now I can show everyone by auditioning for this play instead." I pulled my pillow away from her because she was about to pound the stuffing out of it.

"Nobody thinks I'd be brave enough to do something like try out for a play and be up onstage. It just doesn't seem like something I would do. But I really want to try it. And I can show everyone that I'm not a wimp if I do this."

Molly clutched her head in frustration. "But why can't you do both? Why can't you come to the lessons and do your jump, and then when camp's over, you can do this play? It's not like riding is keeping you from your acting career."

I picked up the blue sheet of paper that was lying on the bed between us and stared at the words. There was something else I felt I should tell Molly.

"I'm beginning to realize something. Maybe I'm not really that into riding."

"Since when? You love riding! It's your favorite activity."

"No, *you* love riding. It's *your* favorite activity. And it's Whitney's and Amber's." I paused for several long seconds. "But I'm not sure it's my favorite. I mean, I like it. But the main reason I started riding was because Madison did it. And now you and all our other friends do it. But lately, I'm not so sure I even want to keep doing it."

Molly looked away and got really, really quiet. I waited for her to say something, but she didn't. The silence of us both not saying anything seemed to suck all the air out of the room.

And then I saw it. A single tear was trickling down her cheek, leaving a wet trail down her face.

"You're crying?" I asked. I totally hadn't expected that. "Why are you crying?"

Molly still wouldn't say anything or even look at me. She stared at the floor in front of us. Then slowly she reached up to swipe away the tears that were now streaming down her face.

"Molly, what's wrong?" I reached out to pat her arm, and finally she looked at me.

"Don't you get it?" she asked.

"Get what?"

"Horses and riding and lessons and all that—that's something we do together. It's something we've got in common." She rubbed both eyes with her fingertips. "But now you say you want to give it all up and start acting. Okay, fine."

She gave me a long look. "But maybe we won't stay friends. You'll be doing acting stuff and I'll be doing horse stuff and . . . what will we do together?"

Now I was the one who felt like crying. "Of course we'll still be friends! Look, I promise I'll come watch you when you're ready to do your first jump."

"But we were going to do our first jump together!"

"I know, but . . ."

"You're just scared, Jordan!" Molly said suddenly. Now she seemed mad at me. "I saw what happened this morning. You weren't going to faint. You just let yourself get freaked out over getting on a horse. You're thinking you're going to fall or you're going to get hurt. You can't let your fear keep you from doing the things you really love!"

I folded up the audition announcement and tucked it back inside my book to keep it safe. "But . . . maybe I can love this. I do get scared just thinking about auditioning. But I'm not going to let my fears keep me from trying out for this play."

Molly shook her head in disgust. "Yeah, just like jumping. When camp started, you were so sure you wanted to do that. And now look. You're backing out of it. What makes you think you're not going to back out of this audition when the time gets close?"

I stared at her with my mouth open. How could she say something so mean?

Molly sat there, glaring at me. "Admit it, Jordan. You're just using this acting thing as an excuse to get out of jumping."

Was I? Did I really want to give up riding? Was my whole life controlled by how scared I got over everything?

Right now, trying out for the play seemed like something I really wanted to do. But it was a whole month away. Just like when camp started, I'd had a whole month ahead of me before I knew I'd have to jump. Now that the time was almost here, maybe I was looking for excuses to get out of it.

"I guess maybe I am a little scared."

Molly's whole expression changed when I said that. "You just have to come back and do the next lesson. It'll be okay. Wayward's a great teacher, and she wouldn't let us do anything that's not safe."

I nodded. Maybe she was right. It wasn't like riding was interfering with acting. I'd have to keep going to activities until camp was over. And if I didn't go to riding with all my friends, what else was I going to do?

"What did we do today, anyway?"

Molly suddenly grinned. "We did a lot of cantering. And we did some work with the cavalettis. It was great. I wished you'd at least stayed to watch us."

"What did you do with the cavalettis?" I asked.

"Wayward had them spaced out on the ground, and we had to practice walking and then trotting over them."

That was supposed to prepare us to jump crossrails. Once you and your horse could trot through cavalettis easily, it wasn't a big step to have him jump a crossrail.

"I'll tell you something, but you better not laugh," I said.

Molly smiled a little. "Okay, I won't. I promise."

"Well, you know at our last lesson, when we were walking through the cavalettis? I had this crazy thought that maybe Odie would step *on* the pole instead of *over* it. I thought his feet would slide out from under him. And then he'd be flat on his belly with all four legs sticking out in all directions. That's what I was afraid of."

Molly was trying hard not to laugh, but she couldn't hold it in. I didn't really care that she was laughing. That's why I'd told her in the first place—to stop us from acting so mad at each other.

I picked up my pillow and smacked her with it. "You said you wouldn't laugh!"

"I know. Sorry." She smiled slyly. "I'll tell you something I used to be afraid of. You can laugh if you want."

"Yeah? What?"

Molly glanced around the cabin. "When I was little, I was afraid of umbrellas."

That really did make me burst out laughing. "Umbrellas?"

Molly smiled. "Don't laugh. They can be really scary. Like, in the wind, they can turn inside out. And whenever I was holding one, I was always afraid I was going to get lifted off the ground and go flying through the air like Mary Poppins."

I was laughing so hard that my stomach hurt. "And I thought I had all kinds of crazy fears!" I noticed the little travel umbrella that Tis had hanging from a nail by her bed, so I went and grabbed it. I opened it up and ran back over to where Molly was sitting on the bed.

"Watch out! I think the wind is picking up!" I said, waving the open umbrella over Molly's head.

"Stop! Don't you know that's bad luck?" Molly tried to push the umbrella away.

"Okay, now that I've faced my fears, are you ready to face yours?" Molly asked me when we stopped laughing long enough for her to talk.

"Yeah. I am," I told her.

I should just do it. Do the jump, get it over with, and then everyone would leave me alone.

What Molly had said still sort of bothered me,

though. She'd really hurt my feelings. But one of the reasons it hurt so bad was because I knew what she said was true.

I did tend to back out of things at the last minute. Right now I was all excited about auditioning for the play.

But how was I going to feel a month from now?

CHAPTER 17

Wednesday, July 2

"Hey, Jordan—remember? Relax your hands," Wayward reminded me for maybe the fourth or fifth time today. All during today's lesson, I'd been way too restrictive with the reins. We were cantering, and things weren't going well. I was so stressed, the whole back of my T-shirt was soaking wet from sweat, and I noticed my jaw was hurting because I had my teeth clenched.

Nothing was going right, and I couldn't wait for the lesson to be over so I could get off this horse. Odie had been jittery and jumpy today. He kept tossing his head up and snorting, and he was startling at the least little thing.

"Okay, let's stop there," Wayward told us. We moved our horses down to a walk and then came to a halt.

Finally. This had been the second worst lesson of my life. It seemed like nothing had gone right.

As we were dismounting, Madison saw that we were finishing up, so she came over to help us lead our horses out of the ring.

"Hey. How did it go today?" she asked. I had Odie by the reins, and we were walking back toward the stables.

"Fine," I told her. If she'd seen any of our lesson, she probably knew it hadn't been fine.

It had been so hard for me to even climb back into the saddle today. I'd felt exactly the same way as I'd felt on Monday—like an eggshell about to crack.

But I'd done it. I had no other choice. If I'd skipped another lesson, twenty different people would've given me a hard time about it.

It hadn't taken long on Monday for the whole world to hear that I'd "felt faint" at my lesson. At lunch that day, Eda made a point of stopping me and asking if I was feeling all right. And then the next day, I'd gotten an e-mail from Mama saying she hoped that I was enjoying riding, but I shouldn't put myself under too much pressure. Then she'd gone on and on about how Maddy and I were two different people, and I shouldn't compare myself to her all the time.

What brought all that on? And who was the spy who

had told both Eda and Mama about Monday's lesson? I had a feeling I knew her last name. And it happened to be the same as mine.

"How about next week?" Wayward was saying to Molly as we walked up.

"Next week?" Molly groaned. "We have to wait that long? Why can't we try a jump on Friday?"

"We can't do it Friday. That's the Fourth," Whitney reminded her. "We won't be going to activities at all on Friday."

We always did special activities to celebrate the Fourth of July. One tradition was to have a capture-the-flag game between the different age groups, and then later we always had a counselor hunt where all the counselors could hide anywhere in camp, and all the campers had to look for them.

"You'll be ready by next week," Wayward told us. "We'll just do a couple of easy jumps over the cross-rail. It'll be set low, and everything's going to be Zen. Nothing to be nervous about."

Was she looking right at me when she said that?

"Okay. That sounds good," I said. Actually, it did sound good. Wayward was right—we were ready for it. We'd been working up to this all summer. I'd seen Whitney do it, and it really wasn't going to be that big of a deal. Once I'd finally done it, I knew I was going to feel so much better.

We started walking away from the stables, but Madison wasn't leaving my side.

"Don't you have to stay and help out with the rest of the lessons?" I asked her.

"Yeah, I do. I just want to let you know how much improvement you've made this summer. You're really getting to be a good rider, Jordan."

She had one arm around my shoulders as we walked along. "Thanks," I said, because she really sounded like she meant it. Madison was so experienced. If she thought I was getting better, maybe I really was. Maybe today had just been an off day.

"You're going to do great on Monday. You're totally ready for it. And it'll be easy. Just don't think about it too much," she advised. "You know, riding isn't just physical. A lot of it is mental."

"What do you mean, mental?" asked Molly.

"Well, like if you've been working at a sport for a while, your body knows how to do certain things, right? Like you're all experienced at trotting around the ring in two-point now, so your body knows how to do that. But you can sometimes be analyzing things so much that you start to not trust yourself."

"I know what you mean," said Amber. "When I was playing softball last season, I got hit in the batter's box twice in one game by wild pitches. After that, my hitting was really bad because I kept thinking that I was going to get hit again. It took me about three games to get over it."

"Yeah, that's just what I'm talking about," Madison agreed with her. "Sometimes you need to just do it without thinking."

"Are you going to watch us next week?" I asked.

Madison looked at me. "Do you want me to watch you?"

"Yeah, I do." This is what I'd been working up to all summer, so I did want Maddy to see it. I knew she was dying to watch me. The only reason she'd stay away would be if I told her I didn't want her there. And I wanted to show her I could do it.

"Then I'll be there. I can't wait to see you!"

At that moment, I was so glad that Molly had talked me into coming back to today's lesson. I was actually going to do it. I was finally ready to jump.

Saturday, July 5

"Admit it. You don't believe I'll do it," I told Molly.

She just laughed. She'd been laughing at me all day about this. It was late in the evening, and we were walking down the hill to the dining hall. The second dance with Camp Crockett was about to start as soon as all the boys arrived.

"I'm going to do this. I'm so sure I'm going to do this we should make a bet."

"What kind of bet?" asked Molly.

She patted her short hair carefully to make sure it was all in place. She looked nice tonight in a loose, hippie-style dress that was the same color as the ocean. I'd decided not to wear anything that would glow in the dark, so I had on a short khaki skirt and a white tank top.

"If I ask a boy to dance tonight, you have to do my chores all next week," I said.

"Not for a week! That's too much."

"Okay, then how about for three days?" I suggested. I loved the idea that for the next three days of inspection, Molly would have to do my cleaning job for me. I hoped at least one of those days she'd have to sweep Side B, because I hated that job more than any of the others.

"Make it two," said Molly. "And let's shake on it." So we did.

"If I don't ask a boy to dance tonight, I'll do your job for two days. But if I do, you'll have to do my job for two days."

"Deal."

In front of us, Reb, Kelly, and Jennifer were deep in the middle of a conversation, and I couldn't keep from feeling a wee bit jealous, knowing Kelly was going to be dancing with Ethan tonight. He'd written her a letter a couple of days ago, just like he'd written me last summer.

Molly knew it had sort of depressed me, so today she'd been bugging me nonstop about how she didn't want me hiding behind her all night, refusing to dance at all. But she didn't need to worry about that.

I'd made up my mind that tonight's dance was going to be different. I couldn't stop thinking about what she'd said about how I'd probably back out of auditioning for the play. What if she was right?

What if I talked about doing it, but then backed out at the last minute?

I really needed to practice being fearless. And the dance seemed like a good place to start. It was like Molly had said, what was the worst thing that could happen?

But the second we walked into the dining hall, I started to get nervous. The boys weren't even here yet, and already I was feeling all shaky inside.

"Okay, you've got to let me do this my own way," I whispered to Molly as we stood around in the crowd of girls. "I get to pick out who I'm going to ask, and how and when I'm going to do it."

"Whatever. I'm really looking forward to sleeping late next week. Try not to wake me up when you're taking the trash out, okay? Hey, look. Some vans just pulled up."

Now the boys were coming in through the dining hall doors. I'd been thinking about my strategy for tonight. People were always saying you should be yourself whenever you were meeting new people, but

I didn't think that was very good advice for what I was about to do. I was not the type to be bold and talk to a boy first.

But if I pretended I was someone else, then maybe I could act bold. This would be good practice if I really wanted to get into acting later. That way, Jordan wouldn't have to ask someone to dance. Maybe I'd walk up to a boy and act like I was Molly instead.

Now the music was playing, and people were gradually starting to dance. I noticed a boy who wasn't talking to any other guys at the moment. He was very normal-looking, with brown hair and a friendly face, not too tall, not too short. He had on a gray Old Navy T-shirt, and for whatever reason I decided that he'd be the one. I turned to Molly.

"All right. I'm going to do it. Are you watching?"

She had a really evil grin on her face. "Go ahead. I can't wait to see this."

So I started walking toward him, but of course, wouldn't you know it, my internal organs started acting up. My heart was racing, and I suddenly realized that I could pretend to be Molly all night long, but I couldn't borrow her heart for the evening. So was this really going to work?

Plus, as I got closer to him, he looked right at me.

His eyes got a little wider, like he was wondering what I was about to do. I looked past his head to make him think I'd just seen someone else I knew. Then I walked by him and slowly made my way through the people lined up around the dining hall.

Okay, that hadn't worked. I was still moving through the crowd when I felt someone grab my arm. "Good job! I'm so proud of you," said Molly with a laugh.

I turned around and faced her. "Okay, okay. So I didn't ask that guy. I was about to. But then he . . . looked at me." As soon as the words were out of my mouth, I started to laugh.

"He looked at you? Oh my gosh, I can't believe he looked at you! Why don't you try blindfolding the next guy?" said Molly.

"Stop making fun of me!" I yelled. But I was still laughing. It was pretty funny. "Why can't I do this, Molly? Why can't I be brave like you and just walk up to a boy?"

She shook her head. "I don't know. Just do it."

I sighed and looked around for my next victim. I noticed that Kelly and Ethan had found each other again, but I wasn't going to let that get to me. Then I saw the redheaded guy who thought I had blisters on my brain. He was out.

"Okay, I'm going to try this again," I said, once I'd picked out a short boy with black hair.

"Good luck," Molly said as I walked away from her.

Stay calm, I told myself. *Don't even think about what he might say. Just do it.* This boy was watching all the dancers, so at least he wasn't looking at me as I walked up to him.

But when I was just a few feet away from him, two other boys came over and started talking to him. So I veered away and made a wide circle around all three of them.

When I saw Molly in the crowd again, she was bent over double, laughing at me. Then she held up her hands and pretended to sweep with an imaginary broom.

Why was I always saying I was going to do something, but when the time came, I'd back down? I just had to do this. I had to show Molly that in some situations, I could be fearless.

So I spun around where I was standing and just did it. "Do you want to dance?" I asked a boy next to me. One second I'd just laid eyes on him, and the next second I'd blurted it out. Brown eyes, braces, blue T-shirt. That's all I saw.

"Uh, no thank you." Then he walked away.

No thank you? No thank you?

I couldn't believe what had just happened! I felt a

blush start at the top of my head and seep all the way down to my toenails. Did I have bad breath? Did I seem desperate? Did he just hate the sight of my face?

Molly must have seen what had happened, because she came right over to me. "You did it! I thought you'd back down, but you did it!"

"He said no!" I whispered hoarsely to her.

"So what? You asked him! That was the bet, and you won!"

"But Molly, he said no! I'm so humiliated!" I covered my face with my hands, and I could feel the heat radiating like a sunburn through my fingers.

"It doesn't matter. You did it, and I'll do your job for two days next week. Now go ask someone else," she demanded.

"No! Not after what just happened!" I still had my face covered.

"Why not? Was it that bad? How is him turning you down any worse than you turning down that guy at the last dance?"

I lowered my hands from my face and looked at her. "Good point. Okay. Maybe I'll try it again. But after this, I'm done."

The next boy I picked out had short blond hair and lots of freckles. I slowly walked toward him, glancing at the dancers so he wouldn't know I was headed in his direction. I planned to act like Molly when I asked him. Friendly, cheerful. Smiley. But then something completely unexpected happened.

When I opened my mouth to talk to him, Wayward's voice came out. "Hey, how's it going? Feel like dancing?" I literally sounded just like her. All I needed was a plaid hat.

I almost laughed out loud over that. Maybe there really was something to this acting thing.

"Um, sure. Okay," he said.

Oh my God! It worked! It worked!

As we were walking out to the dance floor, I could see Molly smiling at us.

"What's your name?" he asked over the noise of the music.

For a second I almost said "Wayward" until I caught myself. "Jordan. What about you?"

"Sean."

And then we just started talking. About everything. About Camp Crockett and Pine Haven, and the activities we did. He was really into kayaking, and I told him about riding. He actually sounded interested.

But the whole time we were talking, I just kept thinking one thing.

I did it! I did it! I'm fearless!

CHAPTER 19

Monday, July 7

"Let's put the costumes on the bench, and then we can sort through them to see what's here," I suggested.

"Are you sure we're even going to need costumes?" asked Molly, dropping the armload of assorted clothes she was holding.

"Yes, it'll be a lot more fun with costumes," I told her. I dumped my load beside hers. Melissa and Kelly piled the stuff they were carrying on top.

Rachel and Tis had sent the four of us down to the lodge to plan something for the talent show later in the week. Rachel had told us we could raid the costume box in Junior Lodge to see if we could find anything. So that had been our first stop. Then we'd carried the stuff over to our lodge to begin making plans.

But the problem we were having was the same one we always had whenever our cabin had to plan something together. Nobody was ever interested in doing it but me. Ordinarily, Erin and Brittany would be willing to get involved, but they were about to leave for a hiking overnight.

Reb and Jennifer weren't around, and even though Kelly had come with us, she obviously wasn't in the mood to do any planning right now. Nobody was really sure what was going on, but she and Reb had had a major fight during the dance on Saturday.

"This is going to be so much fun!" I predicted.

"Yeah, let me know if you want me to do anything," said Kelly. Then she walked out of the lodge and sat down by herself out on the porch.

"Great. She's going to be a lot of help," Molly murmured.

"Don't worry about it," I told her. "The three of us can come up with some ideas."

"I'll help," offered Melissa. "I don't want a lot of lines. But I *will* help."

"I think this is going to be great," I told the two of them. "Usually when we're planning a skit for evening program, they give us half an hour at the most to come up with something. But we've got till Thursday. And we've got costumes!"

"You love this kind of thing, don't you?" asked Molly.

I smiled at her. "You know I do."

Molly, Melissa, and I sat down in a semicircle on the wooden floor of the empty lodge.

"Okay, we know we want to do a skit or a song or something that we can do as a group, right?" I asked.

Every cabin in camp had to enter at least one act. Sometimes one person would volunteer to do something, like play an instrument or do a gymnastics routine. Whitney had told us this morning that she was going to play the violin.

Personally, I thought it was kind of boring to listen to someone playing an instrument, even if they were really good. I wanted to do something fun that would involve as many of our cabinmates as possible.

"Okay, let's look through these costumes and see if they give us any ideas," I suggested. I grabbed a black top hat out of the pile and put it on. "Do I look presidential?" I asked.

Molly pulled out a pink feather boa and wrapped it around her neck. "I should've worn this to the dance," she said with a laugh.

We spread out all the assorted pieces and looked them over. There were lots of old-lady dresses, and some suit coats and hats. We also came across a Batman mask, a black, curly wig, some clown shoes, and some Raggedy Ann hair.

"We're never going to be able to do anything with all this stuff," said Molly. I had to admit, it was a pretty weird mix.

"Oh, come on, there's a lot we could do. Batman versus a killer clown. Abraham Lincoln and a dance hall girl. With all these dresses and suits, we could even do a scene from *Our Town*."

I was digging through the pile when I saw some kind of leopard-skin print, so I pulled that out. Then I saw another one. I held them up and looked them over.

Two leopard-skin costumes.

"No, I got it. How about this?" I said, holding them up for the rest of them to see. "What about a jungle theme?"

"You know, you're really good at this," said Molly. "You can look at all this junk and actually come up with some ideas."

I laughed. "Okay, so there are a couple of ways we could do this," I said. "One way would be to do something with these old suits and dresses, like some scene from the past. I'm not sure what. The second would be to do some kind of jungle theme."

"A jungle theme sounds like it could be funny," said Molly. "I think we should do it the second way."

I turned to Melissa. I didn't want to completely leave her out of the planning. She was at least trying to help us out.

"What do you think, Melissa?"

"I liked it the second way. That's the best one."

"Okay, good. So we've got a theme already. Maybe Tarzan and Jane? And some animals? Maybe we could do a song." *Oliver!* was a musical, and I loved the way the actors were all choreographed while they sang the songs.

"That's a good idea," said Melissa. "Can you hang on a second? I'll be right back." Then she stood up and went to talk to Kelly sitting out on the porch.

Molly shook her head. "We're going to get stuck planning this whole thing by ourselves. Nobody else is even going to be in it!"

"Yes, they will. Brittany and Erin promised they'd go along with whatever we come up with. Once they get back from their hiking overnight, we'll let them know what their parts are."

"You'll have to take one of the main roles this time,

okay? You can't plan the whole skit and then say you're not going to do it because you're the director," Molly told me, giving me this really accusing look.

"I will! I did the counselor imitation skit, remember?" I reminded her, although Molly probably had no idea how nervous I'd been.

"Oh, yeah. You did do that one," she said.

"You know I want some practice getting up in front of people. Maybe doing the talent show will help me not be so nervous when I audition for *Our Town*."

"So you still really want to do that?" she asked.

"Yeah, I do. Don't you think I'm getting better? Did I or did I not walk up to a complete stranger Saturday night and ask him to dance?"

Molly smiled. "You did. I didn't think you'd *ever* get up the nerve to do that."

I gathered up all the stray costumes into one big pile. "I think I'm making major progress." After the first dance, I never would've believed that by the second dance, I'd be brave enough to walk up and start talking to Sean. But I'd done it! And I was so glad I had. It made me realize what I'd missed out on during the first dance.

I wasn't completely fearless. Yet. But little by little, I was definitely getting better. This morning at riding,

I'd had a great lesson, which had put me in a really good mood. We were all set to do a few easy jumps next time, and I could finally write Mama and Eric and tell them that I'd done it. Madison would be watching me, and she'd be so happy for me. She'd have to admit that I was getting braver.

And now this, too—the talent show! We had practically a whole week to get it ready. Things couldn't be better!

CHAPTER 20

Wednesday, July 9

There I was on the back of Odie. His chestnut coat was shimmering in the sunlight, and his brown mane was flying in the warm breeze. I had on a dark green shirt, cream riding breeches, and black boots. My black riding helmet was pulled down low, shading my eyes, and my curly blond hair was in a long ponytail.

At the edge of the ring, lined up along the rail fence, were my sister, all my friends, my riding instructor, and Eda. She was holding up the video camera, and even though I wasn't looking in her direction, I knew she was filming me.

"Trot!" I told Odie, squeezing his sides with my legs,

and then letting up the pressure. We took off at a brisk pace. One-two, one-two, one-two. Ahead of us, I could see the crossrail waiting. I pulled back on the inside rein so that Odie would be perfectly centered.

As we made the approach, I was a little surprised. The crossrail looked higher than I was expecting. For a split second, I felt a ripple of terror run through my body.

Be fearless, I reminded myself. *Fearless!*

Then everything I'd learned all summer came back to me. Don't look at the jump. Eyes straight ahead. Chin up. Heels down. Back straight. Shoulders squared.

I rose into two-point position at exactly the right moment. I grabbed Odie's mane, and then . . .

We were flying! We were off the ground, suspended. Odie's forelegs cleared the crossrail, then his hind legs. We were landing. On the follow-through, I stayed in two-point, and after he was a couple of strides past the jump, I slowly eased down into the saddle.

Wild applause!

I tried not to smile, but I couldn't control myself. I guided Odie around the ring, smiling and blushing. We trotted over to the fence where everyone was watching.

"You did it! You did it!" Molly screamed over and

over. Whitney and Amber had climbed up on the rail fence, and they were still clapping.

"Great job, Babykins!" Madison yelled, and then whistled. Did she have to call me that?

"Awesome. Very Zen," Wayward said calmly over the noise of everyone else.

"Your mother will love seeing this!" said Eda. She lowered the video camera and gave me a huge smile.

Okay. That was a long movie moment, but that's the way I saw it happening. It could be that way. It could be perfect. And even if everything didn't happen exactly the way I saw it in my mind, it could still go well.

As we walked to the stables, I couldn't believe that today had gotten here so fast. All summer, jumping had seemed so far away because Wayward had told us we probably wouldn't be ready until the last week.

But now here it was, already the last week. Today I was going to jump, tomorrow night we'd do the talent show, and then there'd just be Friday to pack everything, and we'd be leaving on Saturday.

"Are you nervous?" Molly asked me as the four of us walked along the dirt road.

I shook my head. Actually, I was, but I was trying not to be. Everything was going to be fine. I was ready. Time for me to make my first jump.

"Good. I'm not at all nervous! I can't wait!" said Molly. She was bouncing down the road instead of walking.

"I know. I'm excited too," said Amber, and then she let out a big sigh. "I just hope I remember everything." She bent down and plucked a daisy growing by the side of the road.

"I think the main thing to remember is don't look down. You naturally want to look down as you're going over, but don't do it," Whitney advised us.

Talking about jumping just made me nervous. I wanted to change the subject.

"After this, we're going to practice for the talent show, right?" I asked Molly.

"Yeah, sure, although I think we're ready."

"But we haven't had a chance to rehearse with Erin and Brittany yet," I reminded her. They'd been gone on the hiking overnight, so it had basically been Molly and me planning everything.

"What's your cabin doing?" asked Amber. She'd tucked the daisy stem behind one ear.

"Jordan planned it all. You know that song, 'The Lion Sleeps Tonight'? We're doing a dance to it. Jordan's going to be Jane, and she's making me be Tarzan."

"I'm not making you be Tarzan. You said you would,"

I interrupted. "And then Erin Harmon's a lion who's trying to sleep, but the monkeys keep bothering her. Brittany Choo and Melissa Bledsoe are the monkeys."

Thinking about our act got me so excited. I'd given myself a big role. Actually, it was the leading role. I was the one who'd be singing the song while everyone else was acting out the lyrics.

Yesterday, when we'd rehearsed, I'd made Molly follow me way up one of the hiking trails deep into the woods so I could practice singing the song really loud. I didn't want anyone in camp hearing me. She said it sounded "amazing," and I could tell she wasn't just saying that.

With just Molly there, I could sing like nobody was listening. Like I didn't care how it sounded. And it had sounded really good.

Amber was telling us about how the girls in her cabin had been practicing a hip-hop dance, but apparently she wasn't in it. Of course, Whitney mentioned her violin playing one more time.

"If we run through it a couple of times today with Erin and Brittany and a couple of times tomorrow, it should be perfect," I told Molly.

"Yeah, okay," she said, dashing about six or seven steps ahead of the rest of us. "I hope Eda's down here already with the video camera. I reminded her at break-fast that today was the day."

When we got to the stables, the first thing I noticed was that Madison and Wayward were standing by the ring with Cara Andrews, one of the other riding instruc-tors, and our horses were already outside, tacked and ready for us.

"Hey, everyone," said Madison. She looked at me and gave me a tiny wink. I was glad I'd asked her to watch me today.

And there was Eda, wearing a short white skirt and her green Pine Haven shirt. She held her video cam-era in one hand and waved to us with the other as we walked up.

"I really need some footage of our expert riders," she said cheerfully. "This way we can let prospective camp-ers see what a great riding program we have."

Molly's whole face lit up. "Oh, you mean we're going to be in one of the Pine Haven movies? I hadn't even thought about that! I just wanted a video to show my mom!"

I hadn't thought of that either. But that was one rea-son Eda liked to take a lot of videos every summer. All during the year, she'd travel around and show movies to groups of parents and kids who were interested in Pine

Haven. Mama had even hosted parties like that at our house.

My stomach started doing backflips the second I heard that. People were going to watch this? Watch me? Strange people I didn't even know?

We all went into the tack room to get our riding helmets on, and then we went back out to start our lesson.

Whitney was practically standing on her tiptoes. "Do you want me to go first, Caroline? Since I'm jumping a course. And then Eda can shoot the footage of everyone else doing a single jump."

Translation: Let me go first since I'm so special.

Molly shook her head in disgust over how pushy Whitney was being, but Wayward said that was probably a good idea. Whitney mounted, and Wayward went out to the ring with her while the rest of us stayed by the fence and watched.

"Two jumps," said Molly. "I guess you could call it a course."

Out in the ring, there was a low crossrail, and then several feet past that was a vertical—a single pole set up between two standards. Whitney trotted around the ring a couple of times to warm up, and then she approached the jumps. We all stayed quiet because Eda had started filming.

Whitney and Cleo took their jumps perfectly, and I couldn't help thinking that this was a great movie moment for Whitney right now. Once Whitney had done the course a couple of times, it was our turn.

For the time being, Eda had turned off the camera. Madison came over to me and gave me a quick hug. "You're going to do great. Just try not to overanalyze everything."

I nodded. My heart was thumping ultrafast, and I just wanted to get this over with. Wayward had taken the pole down between the verticals so our horses would only have the single crossrail to jump.

As we were just about to mount, I told Amber and Molly, "I don't want to go first or last. So is it okay if I go in the middle?"

"It's okay with me," said Amber. "I think Molly should be first, since she's the most excited. I don't mind going last."

"Thanks!" said Molly with a grin. Madison came over to give me a leg up, and I noticed that Eda was now videotaping us. I leaned over to check the girth and adjust the stirrups, but I was so nervous I could hardly focus on what I was doing.

And then Odie started freaking out. He shook his head vigorously and then stamped both of his forelegs.

"Hey! Calm down!" I told him. But he wouldn't settle down. He was stamping and shaking his head like crazy, and I pulled back on the reins, trying to get him to stand still.

"JORDAN!" Maddy yelled at me. And I mean *yelled*. "Stop yanking on the reins! You're hurting him!"

I felt so panicked. Odie was out of control. Maddy was yelling. Eda was filming. Wouldn't this be a great video to show future campers?

Wayward came over and took Odie by the bridle. She patted him a couple of times, and of course he calmed down for *her*.

She looked up at me. "It's okay. Relax. Just relax," she reminded me. "When you get tense, it makes him nervous."

"Okay," I said. I blew out a long, slow breath.

This was so embarrassing! Everybody was watching—Madison, Eda, Cara Andrews. And then suddenly an image popped into my head. I could see forty people crammed into our living room at home, watching a video of me losing control of my horse.

"Let's warm up a little. Walk one circuit around the ring, and then move into a trot," Wayward instructed us. So the three of us started to walk around the ring. Walking was no problem, but when we began trotting,

Odie was acting all wound up again. He was going sort of sideways, and I couldn't seem to get him to straighten out.

"Reins, Jordan. Even them out," Wayward told me. And then I realized I was pulling too tight on the inside rein, and that was making me steer him in a weird direction.

Of course I was going to have another disastrous lesson today! It had to be today! After we'd had about ten or fifteen minutes of warm-up, Molly was ready to go.

"Good luck!" I yelled to her as she trotted away. Should I have told her to break a leg like they do when you're about to go onstage? But would that be bad luck?

It didn't matter what I said to her. Molly took off at a trot across the ring, headed straight for the crossrail.

"She's a little off center," Amber noticed.

"Yeah, she is," I said.

We could see Molly pulling gently on the reins so that Merlin would be more centered. It did help some, but as they made the approach, they were still a little off.

As Merlin leaped over the crossrail, his inside hind leg just grazed one of the poles, but it didn't knock it down. They landed smoothly, and Molly stayed in two-point a few strides before sitting down in the saddle. She held the reins in one hand so she could pump her fist in the air.

I sighed with relief. "She did it. Good job."

We could see Wayward talking to her, and Molly kept nodding her head. Then she did the jump two more times. Both times she was centered perfectly, and Merlin cleared the crossrail easily.

When Molly trotted back over to where Amber and I had been watching, she was the happiest I'd ever seen her. "That was awesome! It's so much fun! I hope I can do it again after you've had your turns!"

"You looked great out there," I told her.

"Thanks. Now it's your turn. It's really easy. Don't be scared."

"Okay," I said, taking a deep breath, but adrenaline was pumping through my body, making me feel like I'd just been plugged into an electric outlet.

"Let's just get this over with," I whispered to Odie as we began trotting. We started the approach to the crossrail, but I immediately realized we were too far to the right of the jump, which put us way off center. If we kept going like this, Odie wouldn't be jumping anywhere near the lowest point where the two poles crossed each other.

I tightened my inside rein to try to correct that, but now we were too far to the left. For an instant I thought we should just go ahead, make the jump.

But then I changed my mind. I tightened the inside rein to turn Odie away from the jump completely.

I could feel everyone's eyes on me. "It's okay," I called. "Let me try it again."

I wasn't even sure if anyone could hear me. This was so embarrassing! Was my bright red face going to show up on the video?

I swung Odie around in a wide circle, and we trotted back toward the jump for my second attempt. But now Odie was too slow. "Trot," I told him, but he was barely above a walk. We were heading straight for the crossrail, but we weren't going fast enough. We'd never get over it! What was he doing?

"Trot, Odie," I said again, squeezing his sides with my legs. He sped up a little, but then he turned to the inside and went right past the crossrail.

Wayward was standing just beyond the jump, and we trotted over to her. "I didn't do it this time!" I wailed at her. "The first time we weren't centered, but this time he ran out of the jump!" Tears welled up in my eyes, and I hated the way my own voice sounded.

"I know. I saw it." She patted Odie's neck. "He's

being a little obnoxious today. He can tell how nervous you are. I think now he's afraid to trust you."

I wanted to tell Wayward that I couldn't help being nervous, but I knew I wouldn't even be able to get the words out. I could feel my throat tightening up, and I kept my head down so Wayward couldn't see my eyes.

"Whatever you feel like doing, Jordan. You want to try the jump after Amber has a turn? Or we can always do it later. Tomorrow. Or Friday."

All my friends were watching. Maddy was thinking, *I knew she'd never do it*. Molly was probably feeling so sad for me. And Eda had gotten all of it on video. Me barely able to control my horse. My two failed attempts. And now me with my head down, shoulders slumped. The picture of a failure.

In one quick movement, I swung my leg over Odie's back and slid out of the saddle. I tossed the reins over his head. Hopefully Wayward grabbed them, but I didn't stop to see.

"Jordan, hang on a second," Wayward called to me, but I was already walking away, walking across the ring, glad that at least my riding helmet shielded my face a little, staring straight at the ground, avoiding the dried clumps of manure, walking, walking, walking. Away.

I heard footsteps running up to me, but I didn't lift

my head. "Hey, Jordie. It's okay. Don't worry about it."
Maddy's voice. An arm reaching out for me, but I pulled
away. "Come on, Jordie. Don't get upset."

I felt like a dam about to burst. I clenched my neck
muscles to hold the sobs inside me. *Eda, are you getting
all this? The worst moment of my life.*

I was at the fence, and I ducked down to squeeze
between the rails, and now at least I was out of the ring.
Walking, walking, walking. Past the oak tree, turning
the corner at the stables, and then on the dirt road back
into camp.

As soon as I made it to the road, I started running.
And I didn't stop.

CHAPTER
21

I was in the one place I was sure I could be alone: the shower. I'd locked the stall door and had the water on full blast. I cried and cried and cried, so glad that the sound of the water splattering against the cement floor helped to drown out my sobs.

I stood there in the stall with the water pouring over me and had a complete and total meltdown. It was just like the summer when I was ten, when I hadn't wanted to go to camp in the first place. I thought I'd outgrown breakdowns like this, but I guess not.

I turned my face up to the showerhead and let the hot water wash over me. I felt like the water pouring all around me and forming puddles at my feet was made up of all the tears that I'd cried.

I just couldn't do it. I couldn't do it. Everybody else could do it, but I couldn't. I choked.

My whole body was shaking, and my sobs were so loud, I worried that someone walking by outside the showers might hear me. But I couldn't stop myself.

Everyone was right about me. Mama doubting me from the moment I first said I wanted to try jumping this summer. Madison giving me that look in the car. *I don't know, Jordan.* Molly predicting that I'd back out of the audition—she'd at least believed that I would go through with the jump today.

I leaned against the wall and cried even louder. My hair was hanging down in my eyes in wet strands, and I couldn't stop shaking. The water was starting to get cooler. Pretty soon I'd be all out of hot water.

I was never going to be daring, or confident, or adventurous. It just wasn't me. I was always going to wimp out. I could never be fearless. I just couldn't do it.

Now my cries had turned into little whimpers, and I was thinking all kinds of crazy thoughts. Like I wanted to stay in here until Saturday when camp ended. Or maybe I'd get dressed and walk down the road past the stables and just keep walking out of camp. I could walk as far away as my legs could take me.

I didn't want to see anyone. I didn't want to talk to

anyone. I just wanted to be by myself, far away from everyone.

Or maybe I should go to the camp office right now and call Eric's cell phone. I could ask him to come and get me. Just come pick me up and take me away from here. He wouldn't ask me a lot of questions and fuss over me like Mama would.

If only I could be home right now. In my own room, with the door closed.

But if I came home early, Mama would be on the phone to Daddy, telling him about how I didn't even make it through the whole camp session this year. This summer, I hadn't even managed to survive. Thinking about that just made me cry even harder.

I'm such a failure. I'm such a failure.

CHAPTER  22

"I'm sick," I said. My voice sounded all scratchy. Probably from crying so hard.

"I'm sorry to hear that. What's the problem?"

I was sitting in the wooden chair in the nurse's office. I was hoping this was one place I could go where everyone would leave me alone.

"Well, I've been throwing up," I lied. "Twice. And I just feel terrible."

Nurse Linda stood with her arms crossed, looking at me very closely. "Your eyes look a little bloodshot. Have you maybe been crying?" she asked gently.

I nodded, feeling like I could start up again at any second. I focused on the doctor's scales next to me so I wouldn't have to look at her. I pretended to be really interested in the weights that slid back and forth across the bar on the top.

She paused for a long time, waiting for me to say something else. Maybe tell her why I'd been crying. But I didn't feel like giving Nurse Linda my life story at the moment.

"Well, let's take your temperature."

She took a thermometer out of a drawer and put a cover on it, then stuck it under my tongue. We both waited for the beep.

"You don't have a fever," she said in an *I knew you were faking it* kind of voice.

Look, lady, I can't raise my temperature at will, but if you want to see some regurgitation, I'm the girl to do it.

"My stomach feels really weird. I might need to throw up again."

She turned around and opened a cabinet. Then she pulled out a little pink plastic basin and handed it to me.

"Thanks," I said in a really weak voice. "I feel like I want to lie down."

"Okay. Why don't you come and rest in the infirmary?" she suggested, so she took me through the door of her office into another room with several cots in it.

I was surprised to see Nicole Grimsley inside, lying in one of the beds with a bunch of magazines spread out in front of her.

"You're going to have company," Nurse Linda told Nicole, but she led me to the cot at the opposite end of the room from her. Maybe in case we were both contagious. I pulled the clean sheets back and laid down, still holding the little basin in one hand.

She looked at both of us. "Let me know if you need me for anything."

Once she'd left us alone, Nicole sat straight up in bed. "Hey, Jordan. Are you really sick?"

I lay back in bed and stared up at the ceiling. "Yeah. Aren't you?"

Nicole laughed a little. "I guess not. She's kicking me out soon. You can stay one night, but if you don't have a fever, she'll make you leave. Want a magazine?"

"No thanks." I'd really hoped to be alone in here. I didn't want to have to carry on a conversation with Nicole, so I rolled over on my side and faced the wall. And surprisingly, in a few minutes I'd fallen asleep. All that crying must have exhausted me.

I was really relieved when Nicole packed up and left late in the afternoon. I hoped no other sick people would come in here and bother me. Could I stay here till Friday? It was only two more days. And then Saturday, we'd be going home.

Sometime before dinner, the nurse came in with Madison behind her. "Feel like having a little company?" she asked me.

What could I say? No. Go away. I don't feel like talking to anyone.

"I guess so." I should've known Madison would track me down in here. She was the last person I wanted to see right now. I did not want a lecture about how I just needed to do the jump without thinking about it.

The nurse left us alone, and I waited for Madison to accuse me of faking it and hiding out in the infirmary so I wouldn't have to face my horrible life, but she kept quiet.

Finally I said, "What's wrong? You look so sad."

"I am sad. It was so hard for me to watch you this morning, knowing how much pressure you were under." She sat on the edge of the bed and patted my legs, which were buried under the sheets.

"You've worked so hard all summer at riding. And I know you felt like it was the end of the world when you didn't make the jump today. But you know what? It doesn't matter."

Her voice was so, so soft. It reminded me of Mama.

And so I couldn't help it. I started to cry again. "It does matter. I told everyone I would do it, and I didn't. I couldn't do it," I said, choking on the words.

"But you can do it. I know you can. We all know you can. You don't have to prove anything to any of us. We all know what a good rider you are."

I shook my head. "I'm not a good rider. I'll never be as good as you."

"Jordan, I'm four years older than you are. You have to stop comparing yourself to me. And you know what, you're better now than I was when I was your age."

"You're just saying that. *You* jumped when you were twelve! I didn't!" I sobbed.

"You could've done that jump today. You could do it tomorrow if you really wanted to. But you know what? Nobody cares! Not me, or Mama, or anybody. We don't care if you jump or don't jump, if you do cartwheels off the diving board, or if you learn to whistle out of your belly button! The only thing we care about is that you feel good about yourself."

I was really crying now. Maddy was being so sweet and acting so worried about me. It just made me even more emotional.

"But how can I feel good about myself? I'm such a failure." My nose was really snotty, and I needed a

Kleenex, but I didn't have one. So I just had to sniff a lot.

"Oh, Babykins, that just breaks my heart to hear you say that. How can you say that?"

"It's true!" I wailed. I gave in and wiped my runny nose on my sleeve. It was gross. But I had to do something. It was either that or the nurse's clean sheets.

"No, you're not. I think you're perfect. You'll always be my perfect little baby doll," Madison said, her voice cracking a little.

"Don't call me that!" I yelled, because that was a family story that always made me laugh, but always choked me up at the same time.

"But you are. When they brought you home from the hospital, I couldn't believe how perfect you were. You looked just like my dolls, but you were *real*." Now Maddy was getting teary. "You've seen the video."

I laughed and nodded. On the day our parents brought me home from the hospital, we have a video of Maddy and me together. In it, she's not quite four years old, and she runs to the door to let our grandparents in, and she's bouncing up and down, and she says, "Come see my perfect little baby doll!"

"We had on those matching T-shirts," said Madison. "Mine said 'I'm the Big Sister,' and you were wearing that teeny tiny one that said 'I'm the Little Sister.'"

I laughed because I could see it all so clearly. We've watched that video so many times. "I looked like a red raisin. I don't know why you were so excited about me."

Madison shook her head and smiled. "No, you were perfect. I thought Mama and Daddy had brought me a real live baby doll."

"You don't really remember that day," I said accusingly. "You just think you do because you've seen the video so many times."

"No, I do remember it. I loved you so much." She stroked my hair. "I still do."

"Maddy!" I said, leaning forward and burying my gross, disgusting, teary face in her hair. "This was the worst day of my life!" I breathed in the smell of her shampoo while she patted my back and rocked me back and forth.

"I know, Babykins. I know. I just want you to feel better."

"I do," said. "I do feel better. Now."

CHAPTER 23

Thursday, July 10

Nicole Grimsley had been right. The nurse would let you fake it for one night in the infirmary, but after that, if you weren't running a fever or regurgitating or something, you had to leave.

"I've been so worried about you!" said Molly when I came back to the cabin right after breakfast.

"We've been practicing for the talent show," said Brittany, waving her toothbrush around excitedly. "I think what you and Molly came up with is great! Do you feel like singing tonight? Does your throat hurt or anything?"

"Molly said you had the song down perfectly," said Erin, sitting on her top bunk with her legs dangling over the side. "So we're glad you're back."

Oh, the talent show! That was tonight. I'd almost forgotten about it in the middle of my meltdown.

I cleared my throat. "Actually, I'm not sure I can do it," I told them. "My throat does hurt a little."

Molly gave me a quick look but kept quiet.

"Oh, no!" wailed Brittany. "That's what I was afraid of! When I heard you were in the infirmary, I said, 'I hope it's not her throat.'"

I shrugged. "Sorry about that. But Molly knows the song. She can sing it," I suggested.

"Yeah, good idea. I sound like Kermit the Frog when I sing," she said, narrowing her eyes at me.

I coughed a few times to show Brittany and Erin how weak I was. "Well, that'll just make it funny, won't it?"

"I wish you could do it, Jordan! It's all your idea," said Brittany.

"I know. But I'll have fun just being in the audience and watching y'all do it."

Brittany left to brush her teeth, and Molly insisted that we go to crafts together for our first morning activity. "That shouldn't strain your *sore throat* too much," she told me. So we said good-bye to Erin and left the cabin.

As we walked down Middler Line together, Molly said, "First of all, I'm really glad you're back. I was so worried about you. I wanted to come see you yesterday, but I wasn't sure if you'd even want to talk to me."

I sighed. "I would've talked to you. I know you think I totally wimped out on the jump, right?"

"No, I don't! You were just having a bad day."

"Molly, how many times this summer have I had a bad day? And how come nobody else ever has a bad day?" We were walking down the hill toward Crafts Cabin when I saw Eda off in the distance, talking to a couple of Senior girls. Hopefully, she wouldn't see me. I didn't feel like talking to her now.

"What makes you think I wasn't nervous out there too? Everybody was watching, and Eda had the video camera. That was all my fault. I never should've asked her in the first place. I'm sorry."

I noticed with relief that Eda had walked off toward the lake without seeing us coming down the hill.

"Don't be. You looked great out there. Now you're in the Pine Haven movies. And your parents have a really cool video of you making your first jump. And my parents have a video of me having my nineteenth meltdown."

Molly clutched her head in frustration. "You didn't have a meltdown! Listen, Jordan. I've already asked Wayward if you could try your jump again, and she said yes. We don't even have to wait for our lesson time. We could do it today, after rest hour. Just you and me. No cameras, no Madison, no Whitney. I'll even stand in the stables if you don't want me to watch."

"No, I'm not going to do it."

"I can't believe you'd come so close and not do it! It's just like Madison said. It's all mental with you. You can do it. You've just psyched yourself out about it."

I turned and glared at her. "Yeah, and why is that? You saw what happened yesterday. It was a disaster. A disaster! And don't you dare bring up that stupid shipwreck, or I'll never speak to you again!"

Molly kicked up a tuft of grass with her foot. "I just think you'd feel so much better if you could say you did it."

"I don't have to prove anything to anyone now," I said, thinking about the conversation I'd had with Madison.

We were at Crafts Cabin, so we went inside. Gloria, the crafts counselor, was glad at least a couple of campers had showed up today. Since camp was almost over, lots of people had stopped going to activities and were just hanging out in their cabins. The counselors didn't even mind anymore.

"We're making lanyards," said Gloria, smiling at us

both and pointing to the different-colored plastic strings lying around on the tables, along with metal clips so we could turn them into key chains.

"Good, you can never have too many lanyards," said Molly. We picked up a handful of plastic strings and went out on the porch so we could talk in private.

"Okay, so you're not going to jump," Molly went on. "But what about the talent show? You do not have a sore throat. So why are you backing out of doing it?"

She straddled the porch rail like she was on the back of a horse. "The talent show was something you really and truly wanted to do. You were so excited about it!"

I sat on a bench across from her, totally focused on braiding together two pink and purple strings.

"I'll tell you why. I broke down out there yesterday. It was the most embarrassing moment of my life. It was horrible! So if you think I'm about to get up onstage tonight and have another breakdown in front of the entire camp, you're out of your mind."

A low, grumbling sound was coming out of Molly's throat. "Okay, then. Forget the talent show. It's not like it matters. Some stupid camp talent show." She paused, and I could feel her staring at me. I looked up from my lanyard.

"But what about auditioning for the play? Are you backing out of that, too?"

I didn't answer her. I thought about what I did and didn't want to do.

I really had wanted to audition for the play. And for a brief moment there, I had actually believed I might be brave enough to do it.

But not anymore. Molly was always asking, *What's the worst that could happen?*

I'd seen the worst. I'd lived through it. I didn't want the talent show and the audition to be the scenes of my next meltdowns.

"Well?" Molly asked impatiently. "Are you still planning on auditioning for the play? Or not?"

I shrugged. "I don't know yet."

Molly shook her head and sighed. "You know, the whole jumping thing . . . I knew you were mostly doing that to prove something to Madison. So no big deal if you don't do it. But Jordan. You should see how excited you are about skits and stuff like that. I really think you should do the talent show tonight. And then you'll feel better about auditioning for the play."

"Not if I get up on stage tonight and fall on my face. That won't make me feel any better. I don't think I could stand another meltdown right now." I'd gotten to the ends of my strings, so I tied them together. I held up the finished lanyard for Molly to see.

"Look, it's okay to be scared. I totally understand that. But don't let that keep you from doing something you really, really want to do."

I didn't answer her. What did I really, really want to do? A few days ago, I knew exactly what I wanted.

Now I wasn't so sure.

CHAPTER 24

I finished drawing on Melissa's eyebrows and stepped back to see how she looked. I couldn't keep from smiling. We were in the cabin, and I was helping everyone get into costume.

"You guys make really cute monkeys," I told them. Melissa was dressed all in brown, and Brittany was in black. With makeup, I'd done something like a Curious George face for both of them, and then we'd used a bunch of dark socks tied together for their tails.

"I'm glad you and Molly planned this for us," said Erin. "It's going to be funny." She was dressed as a lion, in a tan shirt and pants. We decided to use the Raggedy Ann hair we'd found in the costume box for the lion's mane, and I'd already drawn on whiskers and a nose for her.

Molly was wearing the Jane costume and holding a bottle of deodorant that she was going to sing into, like a microphone. They'd decided to cut out Tarzan's part, since Molly had to take over my role.

There they all were, dressed in the costumes that I'd come up with, about to perform the musical number that I'd planned and rehearsed. I really felt okay about the fact that I was going to watch it instead of be in it.

"Just let me take a couple of pictures first," I said, grabbing my camera from the shelf by my bed. Of course, that made everyone else remember that they wanted pictures too, so I took about ten different pictures with everyone's camera.

"We should probably get down there," said Erin, taking one last look at herself in the mirror.

I was just relieved that everyone had given up trying to convince me to be in the talent show.

This afternoon Molly had practically forced me to go to the stables with her, since Wayward had said we could come down and practice a few jumps—if we wanted to. Amber and Molly did do several jumps, but I watched them from the fence. I'd made a point of wearing shorts and flip-flops down there so there'd be no way anyone could get me to saddle up. I really appreciated the fact that Wayward didn't mention my meltdown at all.

Then afterward, we'd come back to the cabin, and I'd watched as everyone practiced the act one last time. Molly had agreed to sing "The Lion Sleeps Tonight," but she sounded horrible. Like Kermit the Frog after he'd been run over by a semi truck. I figured she was intentionally doing a bad job to try to make me change my mind, but it hadn't worked.

We all walked down the hill together. The sun had already set, but we could still see everyone in camp heading toward the dining hall in the dusky light.

When we got down there, Madison and the other CATs were organizing everyone. We ran into Amber, who was busy helping her cabin get their act together. All the people doing acts were supposed to go around back to the kitchen doors and line up, and I was about to go inside to find a seat.

I smiled at them all. "Break a leg, everyone. I'll try to get some good pictures." I left them and went around to the front of the dining hall, where everyone was filing in to find seats.

Inside, all the tables had been moved to the back of the dining hall and stacked up, and now rows of chairs were facing the raised platform where all the acts would perform.

"Jordan! Over here!" Reb yelled, and I saw her, Kelly,

and Jennifer sitting in one of the back rows. Whatever fight they'd had earlier in the week was apparently over now, so I sat down in the empty seat beside Kelly. It felt good to be here in the audience, safe in a chair. I thought about what a major anxiety attack I'd be having right now if I'd decided to perform tonight. I'd made the right decision.

Reb leaned forward to talk to me. "I hear Cabin One's act is all your idea. So I'm assuming it's great."

I shrugged. "I hope so."

"Sorry we didn't help you. At all," said Jennifer.

The four of us talked until the show was ready to start. Then a couple of the CATs came in, dimmed the lights over the audience, and turned on the lights over the platform. As soon as it got dark in the room, I felt a slight twinge of sadness. Maybe I should've taken a chance.

But no. It would be fine to just watch.

Lori Espinoza and Lydia Duncan were the CATs who acted as the announcers between acts. Madison had come inside now, and she was standing by the edge of the platform with the rest of the CATs, helping to keep things organized.

I could barely pay attention to the first act when it came on. Were my friends nervous? Was Molly really going to sing the song the way she'd done it this afternoon? It might be funny, but I imagined all the people in the first five rows sitting there with their hands over their ears.

When Whitney came on and played her violin, I noticed how good she was at performing. She seemed very aware of her posture and her facial expression. She played a classical song I recognized from a car commercial, but I didn't know the name of it.

After she was finished, she walked to the front of the stage and took a bow. We all applauded really loud, because she had been good. Some people were just natural performers. But I obviously wasn't one of them.

"Let's bring on the real talent," Reb commented. I was starting to get antsy. I had no idea when our cabin would come on because the acts weren't going in any kind of order. I just knew I was going to be nervous for them, even sitting here in the audience.

A little Junior girl had just finished playing "Yesterday" on the piano when I felt a hand on my shoulder. It was Brittany in her monkey costume, bending down to talk to me.

"Jordan! There's an emergency!" she whispered. Everyone was applauding, and the next act was about to go on.

"What's wrong?"

"You have to come quick! We need you!" Then she turned and rushed off before disappearing through the dining hall doors. I asked Kelly to hold my camera. Then I scooted between the seat rows to get to the door.

Brittany was waiting for me on the porch by herself.

"We have to hurry!" she said, then raced down the steps and headed down the path leading to the Senior cabins.

"What's up? Where are we going?" I asked.

"It's Molly! She needs you." And that was all Brittany would say. I followed her down Senior Line until we got to their Solitary.

"In here. Molly's sick."

Melissa and Erin were both standing outside a bathroom stall.

"Oh, good! You found her!" Erin exclaimed as soon as she saw me. She looked really worried, but Melissa had a silly smile on her face.

"What's going on?" I asked. I had a feeling they were all up to something.

"Molly's sick!" said Brittany, coming up behind me. All four of us were crammed in the aisle between the two rows of stalls.

Right on cue, I heard Molly let out a long, loud moan. "Oooooh!"

Brittany knocked on the door. "Are you okay? Should we get you to the infirmary?" Brittany's voice was suddenly loud and ultra dramatic.

"No! No! Trust me, I can't leave this bathroom stall for another hour at least." More moans and groans.

Erin turned to me with a frown. "I think she has what you had!"

That was it. I couldn't believe they thought I would actually fall for this. "You guys are the worst actors I've ever seen," I told them all. I banged on the stall door. "Molly, come on out. I know what you're up to," I yelled.

"She can't come out! She's really, really sick!" Brittany told me. "You'll have to"—and then she cracked a smile—"you'll have to go on in her place." Erin, oh so serious, nodded in agreement. Melissa covered her smile with one hand.

"Oooooh!" Molly groaned. "Jordan, you have to be my undertaker!"

I shook my head over how ridiculous this all was. "I think you mean understudy."

Brittany and Erin finally burst out laughing. Molly's hand suddenly appeared from under the bathroom stall, and in it, she was clutching the Jane costume.

"Please, Jordan! The show must go on!"

I turned away from all of them and leaned against the wall. "I can't believe this!" But then I started laughing too. Melissa, Erin, and Brittany were all smiling at me, waiting. Molly's hand was waving the Jane costume around like a flag.

"Do it! Do it! Do it! Do it!" Molly chanted from inside the stall.

Now the other three joined in. "Do it! Do it! Do it! Do it!"

My back was against the wall, and Brittany and Erin had me surrounded. "Do it! Do it! Do it! Do it!" they kept chanting. Even Melissa, as quiet as she was, stood behind them and chanted along.

"I don't want to do it!" I wailed, feeling like a group of zombies had trapped me.

Brittany ran and grabbed the Jane costume from Molly's hand. "Put it on. Then follow us." She pushed the costume into my hands.

I stood there, frozen, holding the costume. The bright lights of Solitary made everything look really clear and sharp. I couldn't believe they'd gone to all this trouble.

"Did y'all plan this all along? Or did you just come up with it?" I asked.

"Just put the costume on," said Erin. "Or we'll miss the whole rest of the show."

I held the costume up and looked at it. The first lines of "The Lion Sleeps Tonight" were now running through my head. Brittany, Erin, and Melissa were all waiting.

My heart was already starting to pound. "Okay. I'll do it."

CHAPTER

By the time I'd changed into my costume in one of the bathroom stalls, Molly had come out of hers. Not only had she made a miraculous recovery, but she was also wearing the Tarzan costume.

As we all walked down Senior Line toward the dining hall, I was beginning to get shaky inside. "I can't believe I let you all talk me into this," I said.

"Don't think. Just do," said Molly.

"Good advice, Yoda," said Erin, and it was nice to have something to laugh about.

When we got to the back doors of the kitchen, there were only a few more people waiting to go on. That's when the cold sweat hit me.

I grabbed Molly's arm, and she looked at me. "I . . .

think I'm going to throw up." I had to swallow a couple of times because the feeling was so strong. I felt icy cold, and my hands were clammy.

"Wow. You're seriously pale." Then she looked at Erin. "Go tell Lydia that if we don't go next, our lead singer is either going to puke or faint. Or possibly both."

Then Molly dragged me away from the crowd toward some bushes at the edge of the pathway where it was nice and dark. "Go ahead and puke. You always feel better afterward. Nobody's watching."

I leaned over and stood there for a few seconds. I took a couple of deep breaths, and then the feeling passed.

I stood up and looked at Molly. "Never mind. I think I'm okay."

She looked at me with wide eyes. "You sure?"

I nodded. "You're such a good friend."

"Hey, come on!" Brittany yelled, from where she stood by the kitchen doors. "They're ready for us."

"Remember: Don't think, just do," Molly told me. She handed me the deodorant bottle to use as a microphone.

"Look. My hands are shaking," I said, holding bottle in front of my face and watching it vibrate.

"It's not noticeable. You don't have to hold the microphone if you don't want to," she told me.

"No, it's good to have something to do with my hands."

"Come on, you guys! Hurry!" Brittany yelled again. And then Lydia was guiding us through the kitchen to the doors that led out to the dining hall. My knees felt like they were about to give way, but I followed Molly through the doors. The lion and the monkeys were behind me.

The lights onstage were really bright after being outside in the dark. I couldn't look at the audience. I thought about riding. Don't look at the jump. Look straight ahead. So I focused my eyes on a dim spot at the back of the dining hall. All I could see was a bunch of dark heads.

Molly, Melissa, and Brittany had started singing the "Oweema-way, oweema-way" part at the beginning, and Erin was curled up in a ball on stage, pretending to sleep.

I held the deodorant bottle in front of me, and my hands were still shaking. In fact, my whole body was shaking. Could anyone see? Did I look as nervous as I felt?

I almost came in too early, but I caught myself. And

then I started to sing. The first few words came out sounding slightly squeaky, but then they got stronger. I could hear people laughing at the monkeys pestering the lion, and Molly pounding on her chest like Tarzan.

But I didn't dare look at them. I had my eyes half-closed, and I pretended that it was just me and Molly, way up in the woods off one of the hiking trails. And so I sang like nobody could hear me.

And then it was over. And everyone was applauding. Really applauding! And yelling!

"Woo-hoo! Woo-hoo! Woo-hoo!" someone kept shouting over and over. I was pretty sure I could hear Reb whistling above the noise everyone was making.

We all ran back through the kitchen doors, all the way through the kitchen, and went straight outside. I sank down on the stone steps because I couldn't stop shaking.

"You did it! You did it!" Molly yelled. "It was good! It was really, really good! Just like you'd rehearsed it! Even better!"

"It was! Everybody loved it!" said Brittany.

"We're so glad you did it with us. That's the way it should've been," Erin added.

Melissa stood beside her, smiling. "Thanks for letting me be in it," she said.

I propped my elbows on my knees and put my head down. "I'm just so glad it's over!"

Behind us, the screen door banged open. "Where's Jordan?"

And then Maddy grabbed me from behind and lifted me to my feet. She had me by the shoulders, and she was staring at me, her mouth open, her eyes the size of two dinner plates.

"You were amazing! You were awesome! You were unbelievable!" She grabbed me and squeezed me. "I had no idea! Why didn't you tell me you were going to be in the talent show? My eyes almost popped out when you walked out there!"

Brittany had a big grin on her face. "We had to trick her into doing it! She tried to back out of it, but we wouldn't let her!"

Madison was staring at me. "You *belted* that song out! I've always thought you had a good voice. Oh my God!"

Everyone was still standing around me, laughing and talking. "I think she should go onstage more often, right?" said Molly, poking me in the ribs. For a second I was afraid she was going to mention the audition, but she didn't.

"Just wait till Mama, Daddy, and Eric see you singing." Madison was shaking her head in amazement.

"Good idea!" said Molly. "Jordan and I could do it for all the parents." She looked around at Erin, Brittany, and Melissa. "We won't have you guys there, though."

"No, I'm talking about the video," said Madison. "I can't wait to show them the video."

"What video?" I asked, a sudden shock rippling through me.

"The video Eda took. You know she always tapes these things," Madison told her.

Video? Eda got the whole thing on video?

"Was it good?" I asked Madison.

She nodded and smiled at me. "It was *so* good! I'm so proud of you!" She squeezed me again, but I was already imagining the scene.

All of us in our living room, the TV on; maybe we'd be eating popcorn. And we'd be watching me and my cabinmates performing "The Lion Sleeps Tonight" during Pine Haven's talent show.

Talk about a movie moment.

CHAPTER 26

Friday, July 11

"You can do it if you feel like it. Or you can just trot around the ring a few times. Whatever you feel like doing," Wayward told me.

"Okay," I said.

It was our last riding lesson of the summer, and we were all warming up, walking around the ring. But at the far end of it, the crossrail was set up. And I could try the jump today, if I wanted to.

I liked how there was no pressure. Nobody was here with a video camera. Madison wasn't watching. It was just our regular class—Whitney, Amber, Molly, and me.

We walked around the ring several times, and then we moved our horses into a trot. I still hadn't made up my mind if I wanted to do it or not.

I'd be happy if I could say that I'd done it. But at the same time, I didn't think I'd feel too bad if I decided not to.

We trotted around the ring a couple of times, and then Wayward brought us to a halt. "Should we speed things up?" she asked. "Everyone want to canter one last time?"

"No," I said suddenly, loud enough for everyone to hear.

Wayward turned around.

"I think I want to try it now."

She nodded. "Okay. Let's do it." She walked toward the crossrail. Molly gave me a thumbs-up.

"But I might change my mind!" I warned them.

I lined Odie up, and we trotted toward the jump. We were a little off center, but it looked okay. As we made the approach, I got into two-point.

Heels down. Eyes straight ahead. Don't look at the jump.

He was heading straight for the crossrail. I grabbed his mane, and then . . .

We made the jump.

A few more strides and I eased down in the saddle. Wayward was standing off to the side. "Very Zen," she called out as we passed her. I could hear everyone clapping. I tightened the inside rein, and we turned around to face everyone.

"How was it?" Wayward asked me.

I smiled at her. "It wasn't that big of a deal!"

"Want to try it again?" she asked.

I shrugged. "Not really. I know Molly wants to, though."

And so for the rest of the class, Wayward let everyone take turns jumping over the crossrail a few more times. I could've gone again, but I didn't really want to.

But I was glad I could say that I'd done it.

It was really sad when we had to dismount and lead our horses out of the ring. Wayward let us feed them some baby carrots, and Molly cried when we said good-bye to our horses.

"I am going to miss you, you crazy horse," I told Odie. His lips tickled the palm of my hand as he took the carrots from me.

We made the long walk back to camp for the last time. "The end of camp is so sad. I have to say good-bye to Merlin. And then tonight, we'll have the Circle Fire, and everyone's going to cry at that. And then tomorrow we all have to leave!" said Molly.

"But let's think about next summer. By then you'll

be able to start jumping a course, like me," Whitney said, trying to cheer her up.

"Right. After crossrails, we can do verticals. And then walls and oxers and all kinds of other jumps!" said Amber.

"Yeah, just think how advanced we'll be by the end of next summer," I told Molly. I made a point of saying *we*, but I wasn't sure if I wanted to keep working on jumps. I could see Molly doing an advanced jump course like Madison at some point. But I didn't really think I wanted to do that.

Maybe. I wasn't sure yet. Luckily, I had a whole year to figure it out.

CHAPTER 27

Saturday, July 12

"Everything looks so deserted," said Molly.

"I know. It's kind of sad," I agreed. "But it's also really peaceful like this."

We were sitting on the hill, just the two of us. From here, we could see a few counselors in their matching green shirts walking around and being helpful to the last few families who were picking up their daughters, but mostly all the campers were gone now. We were the last two in our cabin to leave.

Mama and Eric had actually gotten here early, right before lunch, but they'd been busy helping Eda with all the endless details of Closing Day. So Molly and I had spent the whole day saying good-bye to all our friends and helping them carry sleeping bags, tennis rackets, and pillows down to their parents' cars.

We'd watched the big charter bus pull out of camp before lunch, and the vans full of people leave for the airport. It had been a really sad day, with everyone crying and hugging and promising to keep in touch.

At the bottom of the hill, we could see Madison waving to us to come down. "Time to go!" she yelled.

Molly stood up and brushed the grass off the backs of her bare legs. "I hate to leave this place. I love Pine Haven so much."

"Don't worry. You can come back with us over the holidays, and we can see Pine Haven all covered in snow," I told her. I was carrying *Our Town* because I didn't want to pack it in my trunk.

Only a couple of caretakers lived at Pine Haven when camp wasn't in session, but Eda and her family came back at different times during the year to check on things, and sometimes we'd come along to help them.

"That would be really cool," said Molly. "I bet I'll hardly recognize it."

Mama and Eric were still talking to Eda. Maddy was leaning against the car, waiting. All of our luggage was already crammed into the trunk.

"Thanks for all the help," Eda was saying as she gave

Eric and Mama hugs. "I can't believe this session is already over. It always goes by so fast."

"Yeah, the summers fly by, but the winters drag on," said Molly, quoting a line from one of our camp songs.

Eda laughed and hugged the rest of us. "Thanks for sharing these wonderful girls with me."

"Oh, feel free to borrow them anytime," Mama joked.

It took another fifteen minutes of small talk and good-byes until we were finally able to get in the car and close the doors. I was in the middle this time, between Molly and Madison. Eda waved good-bye to us as we pulled away.

Mama sighed. "I don't know how she has the energy for it. Two more days, and then the second summer session starts up."

"Next year I'll be a CA," Madison announced, "so I'll be able to stay for first and second session."

"I can't wait till we're counselors," said Molly.

"Don't rush things," Mama said.

As soon as they'd gotten here this morning, I'd run down the hill to greet them. "I did the jump. I really did it. Madison didn't get to see it, but Molly did. I did it yesterday." Mama had grabbed me and hugged me, and Eric messed my hair up.

"You did? That's wonderful! We knew you could do it."

But it really didn't seem like that big of a deal.

Madison held up a disc. "I have a copy of the talent show," she told me. "I asked Eda to make me one so we could watch it tonight." She leaned forward and showed it to Mama and Eric. "You guys have to see this. You won't believe it."

"What is it?" Mama asked, taking the disc out of her hands.

"Well, Thursday night we had the talent show, and every cabin does something for it. And believe it or not, *your* daughter came strolling out with her friends and sang a song. Up on stage. In front of the whole camp."

I slumped down in the seat a little, but I was secretly glad that Madison was bragging about me.

Mama turned around in the front seat and smiled at her. "Really? What did you sing, sweetheart?"

"Not me. Your other daughter. She sang that 'Lion Sleeps Tonight' song. And she belted it out! She was so good!" Madison leaned against me. I stared out of Molly's window because I didn't want Mama to see me blushing.

"The 'oweema-way' song?" asked Eric, and he started singing the opening.

"Yep, that one. All this time we've been living with a superstar, and we didn't even know it," said Madison.

"It was great! You've got to see the whole thing," Molly added. "And Jordan basically planned every-thing—the costumes, the choreography, everything."

Mama was beaming at me, and Eric winked at me in the rearview mirror. "Honey! That sounds wonderful!" said Mama.

I was holding *Our Town* and fanning the edge of the pages with my thumb. "Yeah. Well, I haven't seen it yet. I'm sure I look really nervous. Because I was."

"I had no idea you were so talented!" said Mama. "Well, no. I take that back. I've always known you were very talented. We can't wait to see it!"

Now was as good a time as any. I opened up my book and pulled out the blue sheet of paper. "Remem-ber when Daddy took us to see *Oliver!* in May?" I asked Maddy. "I saw this. And I've been thinking—just *thinking*—about maybe doing this." I handed Madison the folded-up paper. Then I leaned back in the seat and closed my eyes.

Madison read all the words on the page out loud. "Oh, this is cool! Way cool! You should definitely do it!"

When I opened my eyes again, Mama was reading

the paper. "Honey, are you really interested in trying this?" she asked, and I could hear the concern in her voice.

"I don't know yet. I haven't made up my mind. Maybe I will. But maybe not."

Molly leaned forward in the seat and looked at Madison. "Don't worry. I have ways to make her do it."

"Stop it! I don't want everyone pressuring me, okay?" I yelled.

"My little sister's going to be an actor! I'm so proud!" said Madison. "I'll go with you to the audition."

"But I might not even do it!" I told her.

"Well, if you do, you'll want me there. You'll need me to hold your hair back for you when you're puking in the bathroom before the audition."

"You're so gross!"

Madison hugged me and planted a sloppy kiss on my cheek. "I'll be there."

It was slightly annoying that she just invited herself to come along with me without me even saying I wanted her there.

But also majorly comforting.

Don't miss a single camper's story—here's a sneak peek at Chris's, in *Summer Camp Secrets: Tug-of-War!*

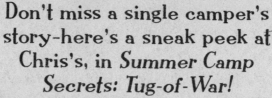

Five minutes. We'd barely been at Camp Pine Haven for five minutes, and I was already tempted to push my best friend Devon into the lake.

We were standing on the edge of Lakeview Rock, this gigantic rock formation that loomed up over one end of the lake, giving us a great view of just about everything from up here.

Not only could we see the lake below us with the wooden dock sticking out over the water and the rows of canoes lined up on the banks, but we could catch a glimpse of the tennis courts nearby, slightly hidden by the trees.

Devon and I had just gotten off the bus, and since she'd hated every minute of the ride here, I decided I'd give her a quick tour while our stuff was being unloaded.

Devon took a step closer to the edge and looked down, her arms crossed in front of her. We were about thirty feet high, I figured.

"I don't think this actually qualifies as a lake. Swamp, maybe. Why is it so green?" She crinkled her nose in disgust, as if the lake had a bad smell. It didn't.

Everything smelled wonderful up here—like pine trees and fresh air. I took a deep breath and got a whiff of wild honeysuckle from an overgrown vine growing around the trees below us.

"It's green because . . . lakes are always green." I thought the lake was a beautiful shade of green, not slimy or mossy. It was the same color as all the trees around it. There's absolutely nothing swampy about Pine Haven's lake.

A group of girls and parents were walking around the opposite side of the lake, and I strained my eyes to see if I recognized any of them. I couldn't wait to see my old friends, especially Maggie. I hadn't seen her since last summer.

Devon let out a bored sigh. "Okay, nice swamp. Let's go check out the pool now."

I gritted my teeth. "Devon, there is no pool. We swim in the lake. I thought you knew that."

She turned her head slowly and looked at me, her

mouth slightly open. The expression on her face looked like I'd told her a gigantic, girl-eating kraken lived in those waters. "No pool? There's . . . *no . . . pool.*" She emphasized each word carefully.

"How did you get the impression that Pine Haven has a pool?" I asked. "Didn't you look at the brochures I gave you? Or the website?"

Devon shrugged. "I might have glanced at the brochures once or twice, but when I went to the website and saw that there was a clock counting down the days till I'd be shipped off here . . ." She didn't even bother to finish the sentence.

Devon was wearing her two favorite wardrobe colors. She had on a black tank top and white shorts. I couldn't figure out why she dressed in black and white so much. Maybe because her hair was black and her skin was milky white. Next to Devon, my complexion was a warm caramel.

Personally, I made a point of never wearing black or white. Too blah for me. Today, for instance, I was wearing one red and one yellow Converse high-top. The best part about owning high-tops in assorted colors was that you could mix them up. As far as I was concerned, the more color, the better.

"Ready to see the rest of camp?" I asked.

"Chris, please wake me up from this nightmare. You can't be serious about there being no pool."

"Devon, are you trying to make me mad? Because you're succeeding," I warned her.

"Ooh, don't awaken the Hulk." Devon knew not to push me to the limit.

All my family and friends were well aware of my temper. My mom was constantly telling me I needed to learn to control it, but I figured everyone else should try not to make me mad in the first place.

"Continue with the tour," Devon said. "Any chance the Sistine Chapel is around the corner?"

We'd started walking through the trees, away from Lakeview Rock, when I stopped dead in my tracks and turned on her. "Are you going to spend the next four weeks complaining about your parents not taking you to Italy?" I snapped at her.

"Yes, that's exactly what I'm going to do. I still can't believe my parents are forcing me to spend an entire month at some backwoods girls' camp in North Carolina when I could be visiting the Forum or the Colosseum with them!"

That explained why Devon hadn't bothered to look at the stuff I'd given her about Pine Haven; she'd been too busy looking at all her parents' travel brochures.

"Devon, you're here at camp, so do us both a favor and try not to drive me insane."

Devon frowned. "Sorry. I'm not trying to drive you insane. The one good thing about this whole camp experience is that you're here with me, Chris. At least the two of us get to stick together the whole time, right?"

I smiled at her. "Right. Give Pine Haven a chance, okay? There might be some things you actually like."

We walked up the road to where the bus was parked.

I'd gotten this nervous feeling when Devon's mom called my mom a couple of months ago and asked about Devon coming to camp with me this summer. Yes, we're best friends, but Devon is not the outdoorsy type. I think she might be allergic to nature. But her parents had planned this big European vacation that didn't include her or her older sister Ariana, so Ariana decided on a music camp, and Devon got shipped off to Pine Haven with me. I really did like the idea of Devon coming to camp with me, but I knew it would take her a while to get used to things around here.

"Okay, back behind those trees at the top of that hill is the climbing tower. It's really cool. Kind of a combination climbing wall and wooden maze with netting and ropes and stuff. And this road leads through camp and down to the stables."

"Stables? You mean, like a barn? With cows?"

"No, not with cows! Horses. You know, for riding. Some people ride horses."

It seemed like there were even more people wandering around now than when we first got off the bus, and I kept looking for Maggie everywhere in the crowd of parents, counselors, and arriving campers. I yelled and waved at Erin Harmon, but we were too far away to actually talk, and anyway, she was helping Melissa Bledsoe carry her stuff up the hill toward the cabins. I was about to tell Devon that we should grab our stuff too, when I heard someone calling me.

"Chris! Christina Ramirez!"

Rachel Hoffstedder, my counselor from last year, was trying to get through the crowd of people still standing around the bus.

"Rachel!" I ran up and gave her a hug. Devon hung back a few steps and waited.